BEAR GRYLLS

SPIRIT
OF THE
JUNGLE

BEAR GRYLLS

NEW JUNGLE BOOK ADVENTURES

SPIRIT
OF THE
JUNGLE

Feiwel and Friends
New York

A Feiwel and Friends Book
An imprint of Macmillan Publishing Group, LLC
175 Fifth Avenue, New York, NY 10010.

NEW JUNGLE BOOK ADVENTURES: SPIRIT OF THE JUNGLE.
Copyright © 2017 by Bear Grylls. All rights reserved.
Printed in the United States of America by LSC Communications,
Harrisonburg, Virginia.

Our books may be purchased in bulk for promotional, educational,
or business use. Please contact your local bookseller or the Macmillan Corporate
and Premium Sales Department at (800) 221-7945 ext. 5442 or by e-mail at
MacmillanSpecialMarkets@macmillan.com.

Originally published in the UK in 2016 by Macmillan Children's Books
An imprint of Pan Macmillan

Library of Congress Control Number: 2016953572
ISBN 978-1-250-11150-0 (hardcover) / ISBN 978-1-250-11149-4 (ebook)

Feiwel and Friends logo designed by Filomena Tuosto

First American edition—2017

1 3 5 7 9 10 8 6 4 2

mackids.com

*To all our BGV team,
who encourage that kidlike spirit
in each other, love adventure,
and always go that extra mile*

BEAR GRYLLS

SPIRIT
OF THE
JUNGLE

CHAPTER ONE

THE TELEPHONE'S CHIRPING RING made Mak look up from the book he was reading on his bed. For whatever bizarre reason, his mother had changed the landline ringtone to mimic the trill of an exotic bird. She thought it was amusing, but it set Mak's nerves on edge. That, along with the abundance of plants his mother crammed in the house, had convinced him that nature had one place: *outside*. Not in his comfortable London home.

He was glad when he heard his dad finally answer the phone, and he settled back down on the bed. But as his father's voice rose with increasing anxiety, Mak sat up in alarm. He went out onto the landing and crouched at the top of the stairs to listen. His father kept slipping into Hindi, a language he seldom used and one Mak had long forgotten, which made it hard

I

for him to understand what was going on—but something was clearly wrong.

Mak skipped a coin through his knuckles nervously, part of a magic trick he had been perfecting. The coin would flow over each knuckle, falling downward, then with barely a waggle of the fingers, it would seem to roll back up. It was a distraction, one of the cardinal rules of magic. The viewer watched the coin while the other hand performed the trick unseen. It was something else his father disapproved of; he didn't understand why Mak wasted his time learning pointless tricks.

He heard the phone call finish and the hushed voices of his parents.

Then: "Makur!" his father called from downstairs, surprising him and making him drop the coin. It was always a bad sign when Mak's full name was used. "Makur, come down here a moment."

Dragging his heels, Mak headed downstairs. The look on his parents' faces when he reached the bottom set off alarm bells. His dad was rubbing his eyes, discreetly wiping away tears. This was particularly unsettling, as he'd never seen his father express any emotion, other than disappointment.

"What happened?" Mak asked with a growing sense of dread. "Tell me."

CHAPTER TWO

"YOUR UNCLE DAVID has died," his mother said with a cracking voice.

Mak looked from one parent to the other and nodded. He vaguely recalled his uncle David, his father's brother, who lived somewhere in India. He had come over to England a few times on business and they had all been out to dinner, but Mak had only vague memories of the man. He certainly wouldn't have been able to identify him in a police lineup. But he was his father's brother and Mak knew they were close, so he did feel sorry for his father. He wished he could think of something to say.

"It was a car accident," his mom continued, when it was clear his dad wasn't yet capable of speaking. "As he was leaving his office." Mak's uncle had owned a technology company in New Delhi.

Mak tried to picture where in India that was. It took a few seconds to actually peg the country with any accuracy on his mental globe, so he had no chance of locating the actual city.

"We'll have to go over for the funeral and to deal with his business affairs," his dad finally managed, clearing his throat. "He has no family out there . . ." He trailed off.

Mak's mind raced. He knew he should feel sad, but all he could think about was a blessed week, or maybe two, without his parents breathing down his neck. A break from his dad's lectures about wasting his time on computer games or practicing his magic tricks. "Well, I could stay with Grandma and—"

"We will *all* be going," his father said firmly.

"To India?" Mak blurted. He had never been there and had absolutely no desire to either. Aside from the food, he couldn't think of a single good reason to want to visit. He was quite happy where he was in London. "All of us? Even Anula?" If his older sister was forced to come too, then perhaps it would be bearable.

His dad wagged a finger. "Your sister is in college. It's important she stays to continue her studies undisturbed."

"What about *my* studies?" Mak exclaimed. "I have exams . . ." As the words tumbled from his mouth he knew it sounded like a desperate plea not to go—he'd never been that concerned about his exams before.

His father's face darkened. "You will come with us! We go to respect your uncle as a family." He turned and walked off into the living room without another word.

Mak knew he shouldn't have said anything, especially as his father had only just heard the bad news. If he had waited, then perhaps he could have come up with better, subtler reasons as to why he should remain at home. He felt his mother's gaze boring into him.

"Why do you always think about yourself, Mak?" she said quietly. "Your father is upset. You should be supporting him, not arguing."

Mak felt ashamed. He hung his head. "I'm sorry. I'll go and make some tea." He hurried to the kitchen, hoping that some chai would help make amends, but knowing that he had a trip ahead of him that he had no interest in undertaking.

To Mak, India was a very big country a very long way from home.

CHAPTER THREE

THREE DAYS LATER Mak found himself standing in the middle of a busy Heathrow Airport terminal. All around him crowds of people dashed past, trying to make their departure gates on time, and there was an air of constant tension.

Conversations with his parents were short, as he was worried that any unthoughtful comment might hurt his father's feelings, so he decided to say as little as possible. However, that didn't stop his father from chastising him at every opportunity.

"Stop running," when Mak dashed along the terminal's moving sidewalk. "Don't touch that. You'll break it," when he dared pick something up in the gift shop. It was always "stop," "don't," or "be quiet," but Mak decided arguing back wouldn't solve anything.

At least he received a smile from the waitress in

the restaurant when he made a sugar cube vanish with a wave of his hand. Unfortunately that just led to his father muttering, "Stop messing around, Makur."

Mak hoped that New Delhi would at least be a little calmer.

IT MUST BE THE LAW in India to honk your horn while driving, Mak thought. There couldn't be any other explanation for the deafening cacophony rattling the streets of New Delhi.

Walking from the air-conditioned arrivals terminal of Indira Gandhi Airport into the suffocating and polluted humid heat had been unexpected, but the crush of humanity on the curbside was even more of a shock. Mak had never seen so many people in one place, and each one appeared to be trying to sell them something—a taxi ride, some fruit, a drink, a mobile phone, or any number of other objects Mak couldn't yet identify. His father cut through them all with nothing more than a stern look and a stance that kept anybody from pestering him more than once.

Mak wasn't so lucky, and several times the ranks of people closed around him, separating him from his parents. For a moment he felt claustrophobic as he was pressed between bodies.

He was spun around a few times until he couldn't see where the terminal building was. Disoriented, he shouted out in alarm, "Mom! Mom!"

Then his mother's hand shot through the throng and gripped his elbow, pulling him toward the private car waiting just feet away. It had taken only seconds, but in that instant Mak developed a sick feeling in the pit of his stomach, a momentary panic. What if he lost his parents? He didn't know his way around the city, spoke no Hindi, and didn't even know the name of the hotel they were staying at. He fought the uncontrollable fear of being alone—alone in a city of twenty-one million people.

CHAPTER FOUR

FROM THE SAFETY of their private car, Mak peered out of the window at the wall of traffic and the pavement crammed with more people than he had ever seen in his whole life, all squashed together. He couldn't help but notice a wistful expression on his father's face—a hint of sorrow, but something else: perhaps a sliver of joy at being back in India.

The sharp cold of the car's air conditioning pricked Mak's skin. Too warm outside, too cold inside.

And then his stomach started rumbling.

MAK WAS PRETTY sure his food shouldn't slither like that. He poked it with a spoon. He'd had *rogan josh* before in England, but clearly they made it differently here. It didn't look quite the same, and the taste was unusual. It left him longing for fish and chips or apple crumble—something *normal*.

Despite his growing list of concerns, Mak kept silent. His parents spoke quietly as they ate but didn't engage him in conversation, and he was feeling too jetlagged to care. It took a few moments of prodding his food before he realized his dad had spoken to him.

"Sorry, Dad?"

"I said we should probably leave you here in the hotel tomorrow while we go to Uncle David's office to get started on sorting through his business affairs."

Due to the time it had taken to arrange their flights, they had missed Uncle David's funeral. Hindi funerals took place as quickly as possible, and Uncle David's had taken place just two days after they'd heard the bad news. Mak was kind of relieved; he had no desire to witness a cremation—but missing it had put his father in a fouler mood than usual.

"That's fine," said Mak. "I'm happy to stay here until you're back."

"You're not to leave the hotel," his father warned.

"There's a swimming pool," his mother said, "and you can eat in the restaurant if you're hungry. We shouldn't be too long."

Mak had zero intention of leaving his room, never mind the hotel. The pool held no attraction. While he was a strong swimmer, he had too many bad memories of being teased during school swimming lessons.

"I'll be fine," said Mak. "I have plenty to keep me busy." Undisturbed time to hone a few more tricks from his book was at the top of his list. And maybe then to order some room service and eat it in bed while watching a movie. Bliss!

AND THAT IS EXACTLY how Makur's initial experience of India unfolded, from within the safe four walls of his luxurious hotel room. Indian television wasn't exactly riveting if you didn't like musicals, cricket, or current affairs, so instead he focused on his magic book and logged on to the hotel's internet to watch a few YouTube videos on how to palm a coin to make it look as if it had vanished into thin air.

Mak began to grow bored, so he walked out onto the balcony. The slice of humid air that slapped him in the face and the monotonous drone of traffic made him retreat back inside, quickly closing the door behind him.

By late afternoon his parents still weren't back, so Mak ventured into the hotel lobby and peered through the impressive revolving doors at the manicured lawns, and for a fleeting second he felt the urge to go outside.

He took a step, but then a voice in his head whispered what lay beyond: heat, incessant flies, endless traffic, and squadrons of beggars. It was a hostile and unfamiliar land, and not one Mak thought he should be a part of.

He accepted it came down to fear. Fear of the unknown, the cold tickle of the unfamiliar. Some people were cut out to be explorers and adventurers, but not Mak. He'd never really ventured beyond the outskirts of London.

If Mak was honest, the thing he feared most was living his whole life within a few cozy square miles and never doing anything worthwhile. But what choice did he have? He just wasn't cut out for adventure. And as for risk? He wouldn't know what to do if he was faced with it head-on.

No, magic was simpler: He could control that and hide behind it.

And disappear.

CHAPTER FIVE

LATER THAT EVENING his parents returned, and the three of them had dinner together. Mak's father spent most of the meal poring over files adorned with the GeoTek logo of his uncle's company, while his mother flicked worried glances at Mak. Eventually she spoke up.

"Would you like me to stay with you tomorrow?"

"It's fine. You do what you need to do. I'm happy here. Really," Mak replied, although part of him felt he could use the company.

"We could explore New Delhi together. It is rather marvelous," his mom insisted. "There's the Gurudwara Bangla Sahib. It's a temple," she added when Mak frowned. "Very beautiful. Or Humayun's Tomb is supposed to be impressive."

"Aren't they just a bunch of old buildings?" Mak asked.

"Leave him," said his father without looking up. "You know how he is. He has no interest in anything—except magic."

The words stung Mak, and he spent the rest of the meal in silence, slowly eating the fries on his plate, which, like everything else in the hotel, didn't taste like they did back home.

So it was a surprise when the next day his father bounded into the room and clapped his hands together in excitement. For the first time since they'd arrived on the subcontinent, he was smiling broadly.

"Come on, Makur, get an overnight bag together. We're going on a trip!"

"Where to?" Mak's spirits began to rise—was this an opportunity to start heading home?

"David's business has operations in the jungle, so we're going to see how they run. I need to get a handle on things if I'm going to take over."

Mak felt his skin prickle with fear. *If I'm going to take over.* Could his dad be thinking of staying in India? Mak felt sick at the thought. Until he registered what else his dad had said. "We're going to the j-jungle?"

"Yes!" His dad's eyes widened with delight. "The wild, untouched jungle! I have always wanted to go."

That was news to Mak. The most adventurous

place he'd ever seen his father go was the golf course. "But there are insects in the jungle. You hate insects."

"We have bug spray."

"And lions, and zebras, and giraffes . . ." Mak was beginning to struggle with his natural history knowledge.

"Not unless they're on vacation from Africa," said his father. "I think you'll be quite safe."

"But . . . but . . ." Mak stammered, trying to think of any excuse that would impress, but his father had already filled one of their smaller suitcases with various essentials, including a change of clothes for Mak. "But I won't enjoy it!"

His father stopped packing, his hand on the lid as he took a deep breath. He angled his head toward Mak and spoke in a low voice, clearly fighting the desire to snap at his son.

"I am not asking you to enjoy it. I am asking you to at least try something new."

"I don't want to try anything new—"

"Your uncle left London and came out here to launch his business because he wanted to try something different. Something exciting! He was curious, and curiosity takes us through new doors and on to new experiences. He came here and created some remarkable things, gave jobs and hope to many people."

"Yeah, but look where it got him." As soon as the words tumbled out of Mak's mouth he regretted them, expecting his dad to shout at him. Instead he just looked sad and exhaled a short sigh. Then he yanked the suitcase's zipper closed.

Mak knew any chance of pleading to stay at the hotel was gone. He was going into the jungle, and there was one thing he knew for sure: He wasn't the jungle type.

CHAPTER SIX

MAK COULDN'T TAKE HIS EYES off the undulating hills below as the Bell 429 helicopter flew over them. The sight was hypnotic. Mak had never been in a helicopter before and was finding it a magical experience, though the relentless throb of the engine had been intimidating at first—even with ear defenders on.

They had taken a plane from the concrete suburbs of New Delhi and, after an unremarkable flight, had landed in the smaller city of Nagpur, where they climbed into a private car and transferred to a private section of the airport, where they found the helicopter.

Mak couldn't help noticing the logo of his uncle's company emblazoned on its side. He still didn't know how large the business was or what "operations" he was being dragged into the jungle to see.

Now, after they had flown northeast for almost two hours, the pilot's crackling voice came over the headset. "We're entering Madhya Pradesh. The entire state forms the heart of India."

Below them, the unmistakable signs of the jungle began to appear. Mak felt his pulse quicken. While he had no desire to be down there among the bugs and beasts, the sight of dense jungle as far as he could see touched a primitive nerve and made the hairs on his arms stand on end. He wondered if this was something everybody felt when confronted with raw nature—an inherited memory from the days when people roamed the lands as hunter-gatherers, relying on their wit and skill to stay alive.

He glanced at his parents. His mother looked interested, but his father wore a grin more at home on a child.

Mak looked back down at the jungle. It was majestic and savage . . . but from up here it all looked a little unreal, like giant stems of broccoli.

After miles of endless jungle, the chopper eventually came to rest on a small concrete landing pad built on the banks of a wide brown river.

They had to wait for the rotor blades to spool down before the pilot eventually climbed out and opened the door for them. Mak was thankful for the opportunity to stand and stretch his legs, but the intense heat struck him hard, and for a minute he felt unable to breathe. The humidity was much more intense than in the city, and sweat stains formed on his T-shirt under his armpits and on his chest almost instantaneously. How could anything live in this heat?

Mak looked around the landing pad, expecting to see a welcoming party, but there was nobody. The jungle almost surrounded them, a vast wall of trees that sucked up the sunlight and offered only shadows in return. He took a few faltering steps toward the tree line, hearing the blood pound in his ears like ominous drums while the exotic sounds of birds and creatures he could not identify howled and shrieked around him.

Don't venture forth . . . they seemed to warn. *Stay away* . . .

The boughs of the trees stretched skyward, and each step Mak took forced him to crane his head. A wave of dizziness suddenly swept over him, and he faltered—saved by his mother's steadying hand on his shoulder.

"You must keep hydrated," she said, pushing a water bottle into his hand. "You need to keep drinking out here or the heat will find a way to get you."

Mak gratefully took the bottle, twisted the cap off, and drank almost the whole thing in just a few gulps.

"So, where are we staying?"

"At the outpost," his father said.

"You mean not here?"

His dad hauled their suitcases from the chopper and nodded toward the river. "We still have a ways to go yet."

CHAPTER SEVEN

FROM THE AIR the river had looked just like any other. From the ground it was a wide stretch of sluggish brown water. Occasional dark shapes broke the surface, but Mak couldn't be sure if they were broken tree limbs or crocodiles lurking in wait.

"The Wainganga River," his father explained as they walked toward it. "We're heading upstream to the company's outpost. That's where we'll spend a couple of nights." He saw the look on Mak's face. "It's okay, Makur. It's an adventure."

An adventure was the one thing that worried Mak. The thought of it made him shiver—and that wasn't easy in this heat.

A rickety wooden jetty stretched into the water, and a long metal speedboat was moored to the side. An old Indian man dressed in a traditional *lungi* and sporting a wide grin welcomed Mak's father. He helped him lift the luggage aboard and gestured that they should hurry.

Mak froze. He'd never been on a boat before, not counting a rowboat in the park. As he drew nearer, the scuffmarks along the hull didn't fill him with confidence. He climbed aboard with a few tentative steps, and their guide tugged at the rusting motor. It started on the third attempt, and black smoke coughed out as they sped away from the bank.

The sudden rush of air was a welcome relief from the intense humidity. Mak noticed both his parents closing their eyes and tilting their heads to enjoy the cooler air. Occasional flocks of colorful parrots soared low over the river, trilling as the grumbling boat engine startled them.

Mak began to relax as they navigated the river's sweeping curves. Trees crowded the banks, spindly branches stretching out into the water as if attempting to pluck the boat from the river. Mak draped his fingers over the edge, trailing them in the cool water. His eyes began to close.

The guide's harsh shout made him jump. He looked around, expecting danger, but saw nothing. The old man was pointing at Mak's hand.

"Keep your fingers out of the water," his dad translated. "Crocodiles. He says that to them you are just food."

Alarmed, Mak snatched his hand out of the water. He saw his father was about to add his own rebuke to the guide's, but Mak looked away, not wanting to hear it. His dad always had to have the last word, and Mak was tired.

Lying back in the boat, he stared upward, looking for patches of sky through the canopy, watching flocks of vivid green parakeets fly past, urgently chittering to one another. Slowly, he found himself relaxing. And, as they continued to weave their way along the twisty-turny river, he was eventually lulled into a peaceful sleep.

CHAPTER EIGHT

THE VIBRATION OF THE ENGINE lowering was enough to wake Mak from his slumber. He looked around, unsure how long he had been asleep. They were turning another bend and slowing as they approached a jetty surrounded by dozens of huts and filled with curious villagers watching them. The air was heavy with woodsmoke and unfamiliar food odors, and Mak's stomach began to rumble.

A heavyset man greeted them with a warm smile. "Mr. Patel, welcome to Kangri!" he said to Mak's father, and gestured around. "This is the main outpost of GeoTek. I am Anil Shukla, chief scientist here, but please call me Anil." Anil reached for Mak's hand and helped him out of the boat. The man was deceptively strong, and Mak was effortlessly lifted onto the jetty.

He caught a shy smile from a girl of about his own age, who carried his bag for him.

Anil then looked sideways at Mak. "So, you are young Makur. Your father has told me all about you." His dad nodded, and several steps ahead of them, the girl giggled. Mak felt his cheeks blush. "This is my daughter, Diya."

Mak mumbled a hello.

Aside from a satellite dish on a pole, there was very little visible in the way of technology. A rooster strutted among a dozen chickens, and a lazy cat opened one eye to peer at him from its position on the steps up to the jetty.

Eventually they reached a small hut, and Anil cleared his throat.

"So, here you are, young Mak. Anything you want to ask?"

Mak paused. "Do you really live out here in the middle of nowhere?" Mak looked nervously at Anil, and instantly regretted having asked something so direct.

"Middle of nowhere?" Anil laughed as he climbed the steps of the hut. It was raised slightly off the ground and made from wood and corrugated iron. "We are right in the heart of the action here!"

To Mak's relief he had the hut all to himself; his parents were going to be in the hut next door.

Diya opened the door and gestured inside. "This is your accommodation."

Mak stepped inside. He hadn't been expecting the luxury of the New Delhi hotel, but . . . there was just a basic mattress, a kerosene lantern that looked as if it belonged in a museum, and a huge spider on the window. Mak shrieked—it was as big as his hand. Diya burst into laughter, which just made Mak feel even more uncomfortable, and his mother hushed him from outside, anxious not to embarrass their hosts.

Mak had never felt further from home—or safety.

CHAPTER NINE

NIGHT FELL RAPIDLY and with it rose the haunting sounds of the jungle, sounding like a million chattering insects. The noise did little to reassure Mak, and he swore the temperature had increased. They were sitting on a raised roofless platform with Anil and Diya as the villagers clustered around, serving them rice and curry dishes straight from a fire pit.

The village elder, who Mak thought looked to be made more of bone than skin, welcomed them to his home. The entire conversation was conducted in Hindi, but Diya quietly translated everything for Mak's sake.

The speech finished with a rousing chorus of agreement from the assembled villagers. When Diya didn't translate, Mak looked questioningly at her.

"He said he hopes the jungle spirits will welcome you too."

"Spirits?" said Mak, his head snapping up to peer into the darkness pressing around them. "Like ghosts?"

Diya gave a little laugh, although Mak thought it was more out of politeness. "People here believe a universal spirit inhabits the jungle. Protecting it. Man and spirit work together to create balance and order."

Mak didn't comment. He wasn't a superstitious person, unlike his sister, who regularly saluted magpies and turned in the other direction if a black cat so much as looked at her, but still he didn't find Diya's explanation particularly comforting.

Diya noticed Mak's constant glances toward the dark jungle every time something squeaked in the gloom and whispered, "Don't worry. They are only frogs."

Mak felt a moment of ease. "Sounds like there are thousands of them."

"Oh yes. That's because there are so many insects to eat," she said with a smile. Mak sensed she was teasing him, so he ignored her and turned his attention back to Anil, who was now showing a small watch-like device to his parents.

"This will lead a revolution in GPS tracking. We've made only ten of them so far."

Mak's father took the device and attached it to a long rubber strap. Anil indicated around the strap.

"This is made from a special polymer woven with solar cells to charge the battery during the day. David's design is unique." Anil's eyes lit up; he clearly thought the world of Mak's uncle. "It captures more light than a regular solar panel ten times the size. Imagine how we could use this to power remote villages. It's remarkable." He calmed down and angled the tracker so they could see the device itself, about the size of a smart watch and embedded into the strap. Only a green LED showed the power was on. "The case is waterproof, impact-proof—even scratch resistant from a tiger! Inside is a very smart processor. It detects movement and orientation and can send a GPS signal in real time, meaning we can track it live from anywhere on the planet." He looked at Mak's father and dipped his head in respect. "As I said, your brother was a genius. He will be deeply missed."

"Who would use this?" Mak asked, turning over the device in his hands. He knew his phone and the car's navigation used GPS to show their location, but he was unsure what the point of it was in the middle of the jungle.

"We do," said Anil, happy to have such an attentive audience. "We attach these GPS collars onto big cats so we can monitor their movements. They are very shy, solitary creatures, yet we can still build a picture of their hunting and breeding patterns and see how we can help them survive—by maintaining green corridors if they stray too close to civilization; or we can try to get the government to set aside more tracts of land as preservation reserves. Your uncle was a proud conservationist and was always happy to support ecological projects such as ours. We test the trackers out here in the wild before the technology is used across the globe."

"Which will continue with me," Mak's father assured him.

Anil dipped his head in thanks. "We have already had great success with six panthers tagged and three tigers. This is our last spare collar."

Most of the conversation had drifted over Mak's head, but the moment he heard mention of tigers, he sat up. "Tigers? There are tigers out there?"

"Oh yes," said Anil. "The next village along reported a man-eater last year."

"M-man-eater?" Mak stammered.

"They have to eat," said Diya. "They're powerful animals and wonderful swimmers. Then again"—she looked thoughtful—"panthers are pretty powerful too. They could lift a buffalo to the top of the highest tree to devour it."

Mak stared at the flames in the fire pit, each charred twig and dancing flame seeming to take on the form of a wild predator ready to tear into him. Then he became aware that everybody was laughing at him. A broad grin covered Anil's face as he pointed at Mak. Mak burned with embarrassment, even more so when he noticed his parents were laughing too.

"Oh, very funny. Thanks for winding me up."

Diya wiped a tear from the corner of her eye. "Oh, we were not teasing you. Every word was true. It was just the look on your face. You looked like a frog jumping on a person who is already afraid!"

Mak smiled tightly back at everyone, secretly trying to make sense of the old Indian proverb.

CHAPTER TEN

DETERMINED NOT TO BE THE OBJECT of any more jokes, Mak went and sat by himself in the doorway of his hut, watching and listening as the conversation turned to business and how Anil received the GPS data from a network of satellites and was able to live-track the tagged creatures on his laptop. Anil then opened a Toughbook laptop and showed them maps marked with colored lines depicting the progress of various tagged animals. Two were even on the move as they watched. Anil explained they were panthers, no doubt hunting in the darkness.

Mak let the conversation drift over him as he sent a rupee coin dancing across his knuckles. He had begun using it in the hotel, as the larger coin was easier to spin through his fingers than the one he had brought from home, and he liked the way its polish caught the light in pleasing flashes. The rhythmic movement from his index finger, down, then up again, calmed his nerves, and he felt his bunched shoulder muscles begin to relax. It was some minutes before he noticed Diya had moved to sit closer to him, legs dangling over the edge of the raised platform, eyes sparkling in the firelight as she watched the coin move back and forth.

For a moment Mak thought she looked very pretty—a musing that was quickly followed by awkward embarrassment.

"That's amazing," said Diya, her eyes still on the rupee.

"It's silly, really," Mak admitted. "Helps me calm down when . . ." He drifted off, unwilling to finish his train of thought.

"When people are teasing you," Diya finished. "Sorry. It was rude of us."

"I'm used to it." Mak stopped flipping the coin and clutched it in his hand. He smiled at her gently.

"You know, you shouldn't be afraid of what is out there." She nodded toward the darkness.

"What, when there are bugs, man-eating tigers, and goodness knows what else just waiting to kill me?"

"People see what they expect to see. To some the jungle is terrifying, and to others it is life. The truth is that the jungle is a beautiful place full of wonder and color. Of course it can be very dangerous, but I have been to the city and thought that just as dangerous."

"There are no tigers in the city."

"No, but animals only kill out of necessity, not pleasure. As my father says, man is the only one to do that."

Mak sat silent.

"The village elder used to tell me tales of somebody who was once lost in the jungle when he was just a boy."

"Let me guess: He was eaten."

Diya chuckled. "No. The boy went missing for several years. They all thought he was dead until, one day, he just walked out of the jungle. They called him little frog, *mowgli* in the local dialect." She paused. "The boy claimed he was raised by wild wolves and shown the beauty of the jungle by a bear and a panther who watched over him, protecting him from a terrible tiger."

It was Mak's turn to chuckle. "He sounds like somebody who was going a little crazy. Perhaps he ate something he shouldn't have!"

Diya shrugged amiably and peered at the dark trees as monkeys suddenly screeched in alarm before lapsing back into silence. "Perhaps. But all tales have some truth in them, don't they? He survived out there by accepting the jungle and not fighting it." She met Mak's gaze and smiled sweetly. "Only when he had seemingly lost his life did he really find it."

Mak blinked. He'd never thought about it like that. Living his life in a protective bubble had seemed like the safest thing to do to live a long life. But what if life really was about living fully? Like the real world was somehow waiting just beyond his comfort zone, ready to be experienced?

He reined those thoughts back in. No. Diya had painted a world of enticing possibilities, but Mak knew that beyond his bubble lay spiders, insects, and man-eating tigers.

Who in their right mind would want that?

CHAPTER ELEVEN

THE CROWING OF A ROOSTER woke Mak up long before the alarm on his phone was scheduled to ring. He'd found the thin mattress on the bamboo floor surprisingly comfortable, and the mosquito net draped from the ceiling had kept dozens of insects, and a small frog, at bay during the night. As he stretched and yawned he felt surprisingly refreshed for the first time since they'd arrived in the subcontinent.

Over a breakfast of bright yellow potato *sagu* and *puri*, which left an aftertaste in Mak's mouth he couldn't get rid of, his father made an announcement.

"We're going to take a boat ride upriver."

Mak wasn't sure he could stand another day on a boat. "Why?"

"To explore, of course," said his father with an uncharacteristic soft smile. "How often do you get to come to a paradise like this? We can afford to take a little time away from business and treat it as a fun family vacation."

"But maybe it could be more fun to stay here and explore around the camp?" Mak asked hopefully.

Anil, who had been sitting quietly for most of the breakfast, spoke up. "It will do you good to see what's out there. Plus I just received reports of some big cats sighted up along the bank. If we could get a tag on one of them, that would be great . . ."

Despite the oppressive morning heat, Mak shivered. The thought of getting close to one of those killers made him anxious.

"A little adventure is good for the soul," Mak's father added in a tone that meant any further argument was futile.

Diya and several of the villagers prepared a picnic for them, carefully packed in woven baskets. Anil organized his equipment, which included, to Mak's great relief, a tranquilizer rifle, and the four of them boarded the long speedboat. The same elderly Indian captain who had ferried them from the helicopter helped them aboard, then took his place at the outboard motor on the stern. All too soon the engine was roaring and the boat shot away from the outpost.

Mak saw Diya wave and waved back—before feeling silly and stopping. She had probably been waving to her father. However, he watched her until they rounded a bend and the girl—and the village—was lost from view.

FOR THE FIRST HOUR the river was broad, and the sweeping, lazy bends lulled Mak again, except this time he forced himself to stay awake. As he did so the sounds of the jungle became sharper.

He saw several circling birds of prey, which Anil identified as kites. They often circled fresh kills, but Anil pointed out that they also hung around the village scavenging scraps, so it didn't necessarily mean there was a tiger around.

Then the river began to narrow, white caps flitted across the water's surface, and their captain began to swerve the boat around large gray boulders poking from the center of the river. Now so close to the bank, everybody was forced to duck as spindly tree limbs swept overhead.

Mak noticed colorful kingfishers darting into the water from the boughs, and the occasional movement of slumbering lizards on branches—but just as he was at last becoming interested in his new surroundings, the encounters were over as they relentlessly pushed forward, as if on some urgent schedule he was not privy to.

CHAPTER TWELVE

MAK HAD ALMOST LOST TRACK OF TIME when their captain began to yell in Hindi and guided their boat toward the sandy bank. He felt the boat rock as the keel gently nudged land. Anil was first out, leaping onto the bank with undisguised excitement, his backpack flapping around his back.

"Come on! Come on!" he called.

Mak's father was next, keeping the boat steady for his wife and son to join him. Mak had been expecting to jump onto dry land, so was surprised when his feet splashed into cool river and his sneakers immediately began sucking water up like a sponge until his toes squeaked together. Sneakers and jeans were not exactly the best jungle gear; he knew that much.

He hopped up onto a boulder, but the slick soles of

his sneakers caused him to slip, and he fell face-first into the sand.

"Careful!" said Anil.

"I'm fine," wheezed Mak as he pushed himself up—realizing that Anil was less concerned about his safety than a row of markings on the bank. Mak could see what they were studying—paw prints clear as day in the sand. Anil was already taking photos with his phone as Mak's parents gathered around.

"See?" said Anil, pointing to a large oval indentation with four smaller ones at the top. "These are from a big cat. This is the pad. These . . ." He pointed to deeper ruts at the tip of each pad.

"Claws," stated Mak. He felt another shiver. The footprint was double the size of his hand.

"Yes!" exclaimed Anil. "A beautiful animal. Big too."

"A tiger?" Anil's mother asked, casting her eyes at the trees.

"A panther. But a big specimen. I wonder if this is one we tagged before. There was a mean boy, almost six feet long, that we tagged a couple of months ago. That wasn't too far from here."

He pulled out his laptop, the screen immediately opening onto a map of the area. Anil tutted in exasperation. "No signal. Our boy could be in the trees watching us and we'd never know."

Mak leaped to his feet and stared fearfully around him. "Maybe we should get back on the boat, then?"

Standing there with wet feet and damp jeans, he hoped he didn't look too appetizing to a hungry panther. Diya's stories of man-eating tigers and stupid boys lost in the jungle were still at the forefront of his mind.

That only happens to other people, Mak reminded himself.

Anil nodded. "Yes, we should." He scanned the trees. "If it *is* our boy, then he may have returned to find a mate." He beamed with excitement. "Which means there may be females farther upriver! Let us investigate!"

In the face of danger, why don't people turn and run like they're supposed to? Mak thought. As they clambered back onto the boat, he couldn't tear his eyes away from the trees, expecting the shadows to come alive at any moment in a flash of teeth and claws.

CHAPTER THIRTEEN

IT WAS AT LEAST ANOTHER HOUR before their captain turned the boat onto a tributary and the river seemed to widen again. They may have moved up at least three more branching waterways, but Mak had since lost count and only hoped their captain knew where they were.

The curtain of trees around them now expanded into towering blocks of green that all but hid the sun. As they meandered along the river, Mak glanced behind and noticed to his surprise that the sky had turned an inky black. Anil sat at the prow, peering ahead. Mak's parents were behind him, toward the back, lying arm in arm and smiling as they spoke quietly to each other, taking in the scenery. Nobody appeared to have seen the clouds. He thought of pointing them out to the adults but feared his father would just accuse him of complaining, and Anil would probably try to steer them straight into the darkness just through sheer determination in his desire to tag another big cat.

Mak blinked, thinking his eyes were misting over as the river around him suddenly became draped in fog. One moment it had been clear; the next, mist had rolled in from the trees in what seemed like a split second. It smothered the light and suffocated the sounds of the jungle around them. Their captain barked a warning in Hindi as he killed the engine.

The absolute silence was deafening.

And then the rain appeared. At first nothing more than a fine spray, then a deluge so severe that what little visibility there was, was halved, and Mak lost all sight of land. With it the chlorophyll scent of the jungle blossomed to almost overwhelming proportions.

There was barely time to process any of this as the water began to swell around them with such force it turned the prow of the boat in a full semicircle. Anil and the captain shouted over each other as the old man yanked the engine's ripcord again and again. Each time, the engine spluttered but failed to catch.

Mak then became aware of a heavy bass rumble, as if the world around them were getting ready to roar.

"Dad . . . ?"

The remainder of the sentence faded away as Mak

saw the mist rapidly billow, as if exhaled by a monster that was coming their way.

Then Mak saw a terrifying brown swell rise up in front of them higher than Mak was tall. Within the frothing stew Mak could see the remains of trees—entire swathes of forest torn up in a mighty tidal bore that now formed an impenetrable wall heading toward them.

The artificial rev of the boat's propeller screamed as the engine finally caught. Mak felt a surge of adrenaline—perhaps they could outrace the wave.

His optimism was shattered seconds later as the boat was lifted clear off the water. Floating debris smashed into the hull, plucking Anil off his perch. Mak could see nothing further as brown water stung his eyes and was forced up his nose and down his screaming throat with such savagery that he was convinced he'd drown. Branches whipped past him—something struck his temple—and then he was underwater, forcing his eyes open to orient himself.

All he could see was a wall of bubbles, tinged with blood from his temple. The dark shadow of a tree rushed like a freight train—then the overturned hull of the boat rose before him like a shark.

Mak instinctively lashed out with his feet and legs to move away from the boat—a reaction that saved his life as the still-revolving propeller passed so close the water vortex in its trail felt like a slap to the face.

With his chest cramping, lungs still filled with water, Mak kicked for what he hoped was the surface.

Then his head emerged from the torrent and he belched out water before sucking in air. Mak reached for a huge floating branch and snagged a limb. It was just enough to keep him above the writhing river's surface. He saw his parents clinging to a log farther downstream and looking frantically about them.

But it was over in a moment. The branch he was holding spun—and a sturdy spur emerged from the water and cracked Mak firmly on the head.

Everything became dark, and the sounds of thundering water faded to a whisper.

And then there was nothing.

CHAPTER FOURTEEN

IT FELT AS IF SOMETHING WERE PLAYING percussion on his brain, creating a dull rhythmic headache that attacked every side of Mak's skull at the same time.

It hurt to open his eyes, so he tried to focus on the sounds around him. Everything seemed unnaturally still, but perhaps that was just the effects of his headache. He licked his lips, which felt as dry as sandpaper; in fact his whole mouth was parched, and a nagging inner voice warned him that he was desperately thirsty.

Mak sat upright. He could feel rain on his face. He forced his eyes open and then lifted his head to capture what raindrops he could in his open mouth, but it wasn't enough to conquer his thirst.

The ground squelched underfoot and he noticed that he had lost not only one sneaker but a sock too.

He wriggled his toes in the muddy pool of water, then bent down and cupped his hands to fill them. He raised the water to his mouth but hesitated to actually drink it—it was pitch black.

And something was moving in it!

With a shriek Mak dropped the water, watching it splash at his feet . . . which was when he noticed the black slugs attached to one of them. In disgust he raised it to knock them off—and saw they were not slugs but leeches the size of his thumb. As he stared in shock at them he could see that they were swelling as they filled with his blood.

"URGH!" he yelled, although the sound was little more than a wheeze in his dry throat. Fighting his natural revulsion to anything slimy, Mak grabbed a leech between his thumb and forefinger. It took him several attempts to rally the courage to actually pluck the parasite off, but he did it at last, in one swift movement, pretending he was pulling off a particularly stubborn Band-Aid.

That sent Mak off into further fits of screaming. It hadn't hurt—like all good surgeons, the leech had administered a dose of anaesthetic to numb its victim. However, Mak's action had torn the leech in half—leaving its wriggling severed head still attached to his foot while he held the sac-like body in his fingers as it oozed his own blood across his palm.

"OH, COME ON!" he hoarsely yelled to the trees

as he chucked the body away, frantically wiping his fingers on his jeans. There were two more leeches gorging themselves on his foot, but unsure how to detach them properly, Mak forced himself to try to just ignore them. Water—that was the priority.

He looked around, hoping to see the river, but the waters that had dumped him here had long since receded, leaving only a trail of mud and broken branches. From his headache he judged he had been unconscious for several hours. It had been late afternoon when the storm hit, so Mak reasoned the sunlight now spearing through the tree canopy and gray clouds more likely indicated that it was a brand-new day.

He had spent the night alone in the jungle.

CHAPTER FIFTEEN

MAK'S THOUGHTS TURNED TO HIS PARENTS, a wave of concern making his body shiver. It was quickly tamped down by a more primeval instinct: survival. With no water in sight to drink, his attention was drawn to the plants on the jungle floor. Forced to battle for light and moisture from the trees towering above, the lower foliage had broad leaves that captured rainwater, streaming it to their funnel-like tips, where it dripped to the root below.

Mak headed to the nearest bush—and tripped several times, splashing into the muddy water on his hands and knees. His bare foot hurt every time he stepped on a sharp twig, while his wet sneaker slipped off everything it touched.

He crawled to the nearest plant and angled the leaf to channel the water into his mouth. It tasted delicious. Back home, Mak had always been baffled by different brands of water for sale in the supermarket, never considering it tasted of much. But out here, deprived of the precious liquid, each drop tasted like nectar. But he needed more.

Mak noticed that the inner part of the plant, where the leaves met the stem, held a pool of water. He tore a few outer leaves away so he could access it. The tiny pool provided more than a mouthful of water, and with each gulp he felt the ache in his head easing. He pulled a few more leaves away and drank deeply. And immediately felt something in his mouth that shouldn't have been there.

Reflexively he spat it out—and saw a small frog. It must have been living in the pool. Mak felt a ripple of nausea—he'd almost swallowed it! The frog seemed none the worse for wear and hopped off across the leaf, vanishing into the denser foliage behind them.

Mak tried to ignore the strands of frogspawn he noticed clinging to the stem and just hoped he hadn't eaten any of it. With that same thought his stomach rumbled.

"Right," he said to himself, finally finding his voice. He'd never been one to talk to himself, yet out here the sound of something familiar helped calm his nerves. No doubt people were looking for him, so he needed to make sure he stayed alive. And somehow let them know where he was.

Like his parents. Were they alive too, or . . . ?

Mak shuddered and forced the thought from his mind. He recalled the last thing he'd seen before losing consciousness: his parents clinging to a log above the water. They had looked, if not safe, then at least secure.

"HELLO?" he shouted. "ANYBODY THERE?"

His voice fell flat, absorbed by the dense greenery. Mak strained to listen for any faint answer.

There was nothing.

CHAPTER SIXTEEN

"ANYBODY OUT THERE?"

Mak listened, and once more the world failed to respond. Mak felt a lump rise in his throat. Was he really alone? No. That was impossible in this day and age, he assured himself. He'd been swept away by the river . . . yet there was no river here. It was reasonable that a monsoon storm had swelled the river and dumped him here. It happened back home, and he remembered enough from his geography lessons to know that monsoon rains could last for months and be incredibly fierce.

The mud and debris dumped by the river made a clear tidemark against the jungle's greenery, so all he had to do was follow it back to the river. Simple.

Mak had imagined the jungle floor to be solid, laced with pathways exactly as he'd seen in films, but the undergrowth here had different ideas. At times he was up to his waist in tangles of branches or stalks of grass that had edges as sharp as blades. Other times it was mud so deep that it sucked him in up to his knees before he panicked and hauled himself out with the assistance of a tree limb.

After . . . ten minutes?—Mak couldn't quite tell since his watch and phone had gone with his lone sneaker—he had covered only a couple hundred feet. When he looked back it was almost impossible to tell one bit of the jungle from another.

"This is stupid," he mumbled to himself. "Where's the river gone?"

A quick check of his feet revealed that the leeches had dropped off, but his foot was covered in a network of scratches from the twigs. Mak decided that was still preferable to walking with one loose sneaker that slipped off everything he stood on, so he removed the offending footwear and sock, which he rinsed out—and almost threw up at the rank smell coming from the water oozing from his sock. Who knew feet could smell so bad?

He tossed them both away before continuing. Then stopped and returned to retrieve them. He had no idea why, but some instinct told him they might be useful.

Now barefoot, Mak was surprised that he made quicker progress across the uneven ground. It wasn't pleasant, but he was certain he wouldn't have to get used to it.

When he could see the sun poking from gaps in the rain clouds, it was almost directly overhead. Midday. While the rain continued in a steady patter, the heat and humidity rose so dramatically Mak didn't know if his clothes were wet from the rain or from sweat.

He had been sure that he was following the detritus of the swollen river, but now that he looked again he reasoned that it could just be how the jungle looked all the time.

One thing was clear: There was still no river.

CHAPTER SEVENTEEN

MAK CLAMBERED UP a tall fallen tree that had tilted forty-five degrees, the tip hanging dramatically above the forest floor. With his arms extended for balance, he struggled up the slope. The top didn't come close to peering over the tree canopy, and added very little to his overall view, yet he felt safer off the forest floor.

"MOM? DAD?" He tilted his head back and closed his eyes, focusing on the vaguest response. "ANY-BODY! CAN YOU HEAR ME?"

Then it came—a distant rustle in the trees. He twisted his head this way and that until he pin-pointed the direction. There was definitely movement!

"ANIL?" Mak half slid down the trunk, falling off at the bottom. A bushy plant cushioned his fall and he began running toward the source of the noise.

"I'M HERE! I CAN HEAR YOU!" He waved his arms. "COME AND GET ME!" He regretted not learning basic Hindi phrases—particularly "*Please* help me!"

The trees ahead shuddered—and Mak stopped in his tracks. Whatever had moved them seemed big . . . and nobody was shouting back in any language. There was a snort—and a deep exhalation of breath from something definitely not human-sized. Mak tried to remember what was out here—not gorillas, not orangutans . . . but elephants, panthers, bears, tigers . . .

Twigs broke as the *thing* shifted its weight. Could it see him? Was it sizing him up for a pint-size snack?

Mak turned around and, as softly as he could, went back in the opposite direction. He didn't care what direction that was, as long as it was away from the unseen menace.

Scurrying through the undergrowth sent Mak tripping more times than he cared to count. Branches whipped his face and thorns grazed his arms, forcing him to slow down to pick his path through the tangle of branches and gnarled roots with more care.

In his rush to increase distance between himself and the unseen menace, Mak had bolted without any thought of the direction he was headed. Reasoning he couldn't get any more lost than he already was, and with the danger far behind, he chided himself for being such a coward. With a deep breath he calmed his nerves and made a mental promise not to act so rashly next time. With no clues to point him in the right direction, Mak pressed onward.

He didn't know what else to do but keep moving.

AS THE DAY WORE ON, Mak's stomach rumbled with increasing frequency and the humidity gnawed at his strength. He made regular stops to drink water from the plants, double-checking for frogs and insects first.

The landscape around him didn't ever seem to change and Mak could have been walking in circles for all he knew. His plaintive cries for help became less regular, as he feared attracting the attention of whatever beastly killers lurked in the shadows.

A sudden familiar trill from close by made his pulse quicken—and for a moment he thought it was the stupid home phone ringtone his mother had set, the sound ready to pluck him from the depths of this nightmare as it always did in films. But this was no dream, and the sound came from a small bird with flecks of red plumage, which looked at Mak with interest before giving a last chirp and flying off.

For the first time the thought came: *What if no-body is looking for me?*

The mere words, expressed in his own head, filled him with so much dread that his legs began to shake.

He sat on a log as dark thoughts swamped him without warning.

Do they think I'm dead? Will they still search for me if they do? Or did everybody in the boat die? Mom and Dad . . . ?

No . . .

CHAPTER EIGHTEEN

MAK WAS ALONE.

That he couldn't argue. Alone . . . but *alive*. And if he was alive there was every reason to believe the others were too. Perhaps they were just as lost as he was.

Peering through the occasional gaps in the trees, it was easy to believe that civilization lay just beyond, and Mak couldn't help shake the feeling that he'd suddenly see the top of a bus pass by and discover he was a few feet away from a busy road . . . but it was just his imagination's wishful thinking.

Exhausted, Mak stopped to sit on a log that was dry and brittle to the touch. He strained to listen for any noises that might hint of rescue.

Nothing stirred.

Except Mak's stomach. He gently rubbed it as it grumbled again. It was so frustrating. There must be plenty to eat around him . . . if only he could identify it. As Mak thought of food, a searing pain suddenly shot through his leg. Looking down he saw ants crawling over his jeans. The entire log was filled with them—not so much a log as an ant refuge.

And these were no normal ants: They were half the size of his thumb, with jaws so large he could see them extend wide before biting into his skin.

Howling in pain, Mak jumped off the log, rubbing every part of his body to swat the brutal pests away, but not before they had inflicted a dozen more injuries, each leaving a nasty red welt that itched like crazy.

Mak splashed muddy water over the bites, but that did nothing to relieve them. He knew leaves helped soothe pain, so he tore a soft leaf from a vine and rubbed his wound. But instead of soothing his skin, the tiny hairs in the leaf inflamed it—leaving a red rash that looked like a burn.

"Come on!" he snapped at himself in desperation. "Stop being an idiot. This is real. This is happening." He tried to think of the books he'd read and the survival shows he'd half-watched on TV—there must have been plenty of survival tips in those, yet nothing now came to mind.

"Food," he said aloud. "Water . . . check, food . . . shelter . . ." He wasn't sure about the last item on his survival list—after all, he'd spent the night unconscious in the outdoors—but he knew he'd have to get out of the rain and try to dry off at some point. His stomach growled again to emphasize point two. "Okay, food."

He began with an initial survey of his immediate area, diligently checking each shrub and branch for something resembling fruit, berries, or nuts. He discovered several colorful flowers—orchids perhaps—but nothing more. Desperate, he plucked a leaf from a shrub, taking care it wasn't the one he'd applied to his bites.

He cautiously sniffed it. It smelled exactly like it looked—green. He nibbled the end and an acrid taste flooded his mouth. It was so bitter he spat it out and then immediately gagged.

Mak was getting more desperate.

Feeling more sorry for himself than ever before, Mak took refuge under a huge fallen tree that had wedged itself against another as it fell, preventing it from striking the ground. A thick carpet of moss now hugged the trunk, and a variety of plants had made their home among the cracks in the bark, but most importantly it offered protection from the driving rain. A broad rock underneath it served as a raised platform above the damp forest floor.

Mak sat there, tightly hugging his knees. The patter of rain was hypnotic and he felt his eyelids closing. Before he knew it he nodded off into a deep sleep.

CHAPTER NINETEEN

A BOOM OF THUNDER woke Mak with a jolt. His eyes snapped open and he was instantly aware of his surroundings. He didn't know how long he'd been asleep, but the fading light indicated it had been for a couple of hours. Another volley of lightning flashed overhead, followed seconds later by thunder that sounded more aggressive than anything Mak could remember hearing before.

He knew standing under a tree in a lightning storm was the worst thing he could do—but in the middle of a jungle he had little choice. He couldn't remember why it was dangerous—but that question was answered moments later as another flash of lightning struck overhead.

The bang was deafening. Then the half-rotted limb the lightning had struck several stories above him fell.

It was the size of a motorbike and would have killed him if he hadn't been cowering under the fallen tree. Instead, the branch smashed to the ground only feet from his shelter—accompanied by a horrific noise— and shattered into multiple splinters.

Then the gentle sound of rain resumed and all was calm once again. Except Mak, who was still clutching his legs and trembling in fear.

It was several long moments later when he realized that it would soon be dark. The thought filled him with fresh fears. He needed a fire. Rummaging through his pockets he produced his shiny coin and a plastic spoon he had absently pocketed in the hotel over breakfast the previous morning.

Along with his wet sock and single trainer, Mak probably had the worst survival kit in history.

He dabbed his palm over his clothes. They felt as wet now as they had when he'd first gained consciousness. He stripped his clothes off, still managing to feel embarrassed in case anyone suddenly came to his rescue and found him naked. Then he wrung them out as hard as he could and was amazed at the torrent of water he managed to expel. But still they were damp to the touch. He hung them on twigs and hoped they'd dry in the hot, humid air.

His body was damp all over and, aware of the smell from his feet and armpits, Mak tore a handful of dried moss from under the log. Checking there were no bugs inside, he diligently wiped down his body. The moss was surprisingly absorbent and scrubbed away layers of filth.

Next he assembled a pile of twigs and leaves from the floor of his shelter. Miraculously they were dry. He made a small pyramid of twigs and placed the leaves inside. He found two sticks. Using the broad one as a base, he put the tip of the thinner twig against it and furiously rubbed his hands back and forth, rotating the twig just as he'd seen people do before in films.

Nothing happened. With growing frustration, Mak rubbed the twig until his palms became bloody, yet there wasn't even a hint of smoke.

"Cavemen could do this. Why can't I?" he roared.

Determined not to give up, Mak ventured beyond his shelter. The rain was just as heavy and the light was rapidly diminishing. He prodded around some dry-looking nooks for more kindling. He found some more dry moss and several interesting mushrooms the size of his hand. He considered eating them . . . but was convinced he'd probably die on the spot, so left them alone.

As he returned to his shelter he suddenly noticed something in the mud: paw prints. They looked the same as the ones Anil had excitedly shown them on the shore the day before. Mak suddenly felt his heart beating with fear. He hadn't noticed the prints before; had he simply overlooked them, or were they freshly made, indicating there was a predator prowling around?

He darted back to his shelter, convinced every rustle and faint crack of a twig was a big cat ready to pounce. He dried himself off again, then added the moss to his would-be fire and began rubbing the twig, building the friction heat between the wood.

Still nothing happened.

Silent tears of frustration ran down his cheeks as he pressed the sticks harder and faster until he eventually lashed out, scattering them in utter disgust. He couldn't even create a fire, the basic building block of civilization. How was he supposed to survive another night in the wild?

Mak pressed himself into the shelter's smallest space, and wrapped his arms around his legs. Despite the warm air, he shivered.

He took the coin and began rolling it through his fingers. It was such an ingrained activity for him that he wasn't consciously aware he was doing it, yet it was something familiar and soothing.

He stared into space and wondered where his parents were and what they were thinking. He hadn't heard the sound of any aircraft, but surely a search party must be under way. Perhaps they couldn't fly in the storm? Yes, that must be it. They'd come tomorrow. He'd wake up and this nightmare would be over.

He suddenly became aware of a creature standing in the shadows watching him. But, strangely, Mak felt no fear.

How long it had been there, Mak couldn't tell—yet the animal stood silently regarding him with piercing blue eyes.

It was a wolf, head bowed in the rain as it stared at him. Its mouth hung open, revealing a range of deadly incisors that Mak had no doubt could effortlessly tear him apart, but even they failed to draw his attention. What did was the tiny bundle of fur hanging from the creature's jaws.

A dead wolf pup.

Mak didn't move. He didn't even dare breathe . . .

CHAPTER TWENTY

MAK'S FIRST THOUGHT was that the wolf had killed the poor pup and he was about to become its next victim. Then he realized that the beast was not staring at *him* but at the coin glinting as it played through his hands. His fingers were moving on autopilot now and he dared not stop, fearing that doing so would trigger a frenzied attack.

Into Mak's head came a brief spark at the thought of what his father would say if he saw him dazzling a wolf with his magic trick. *Not* such a waste of time now, eh?

The wolf gently laid its baby on the floor and nosed it, issuing a heartbreaking mournful whine. The wolf's tongue licked the pup, but the tiny creature did not stir.

Mak was so wrapped up in the scene that he didn't

notice the coin slip from his fingers until it landed, spinning, on the rock floor. The metallic whirling noise caused the wolf's head to snap back up, and they both watched as the rupee rotated, catching the dying light before finally flip-flopping to a standstill, heads side up.

Heads you die, thought Mak as the wolf stepped forward and sniffed the coin. Then she turned her attention to Mak, her wet nose snuffling all over him. He froze as the wolf circled him. To his mind, each heave of its mighty lungs sounded like a hungry rumble. He didn't move, even as the tangled gray-and-white fur of the wolf's body rubbed his bare skin, leaving behind the distinctive scent of wet dog.

Mak still didn't feel the fear he expected to feel—but he noticed that every cell of his body was primed and alert. Was he just too tired to care about death or was there something reassuring to him about the presence of another living being—however deadly it could potentially be?

Then, to Mak's astonishment, the wolf padded away from him, moving off into the thickest of shadows. It paused and looked back at its pup . . . then up to Mak. For the first time, their eyes met and Mak caught his breath. The animal's steely blue eyes looked almost human and he felt a wave of sorrow issuing from the creature.

Mak also sensed a curiosity, as if the animal wanted

him to follow. He knew that was nonsense, merely his own deep longing. Yet the wolf took a few steps, then stopped again and regarded him.

Every fiber in Mak's body urged him to follow, although the sensible voice in his head, sounding much like his father's, yelled at him to stay in his shelter and not follow a vicious predator into the stormy darkness.

Yet there was something in the way the wolf watched him that forced Mak to silence the foreboding thoughts.

He slowly extended his hand for the rupee. The wolf watched as he slipped it back into his palm. Then he rose to his feet as best he could, which meant he was stooped over. He expected the movement would cause the wolf to run. It didn't. The wolf just studied him with the same look of curiosity.

"Good . . . wolf," he muttered in the most soothing tone he could manage.

He grabbed his clothes, which were still just as damp as when he'd hung them out to dry, and quickly slid them on. He pocketed the plastic spoon and his single sneaker, then nodded at the wolf.

"I'm ready."

Mak felt a thrill as the wolf lazily turned and walked off into the darkness. Mak cast one last sad look at the dead pup, then nervously followed at a safe distance.

THE WOLF TROTTED DOWN a narrow trail that Mak had failed to notice in the daylight. The floor had been smoothed by the passing of generations of animals, and the overhanging branches were easily cast aside. Still, in the twilight it was proving difficult for Mak to keep up and his feet were throbbing and sore from stepping on what felt like every stone and sharp twig in the jungle.

He still couldn't shake the thought that the wolf was leading him into some trap, perhaps bringing him back to an entire pack of slavering killers. And, aside from for company, he didn't really know why he was following. But he just couldn't stop himself.

Several times the wolf patiently halted and waited for him to catch up, forcing Mak to draw ever closer as complete darkness descended. At last the wolf reached what looked like a small cave, only as high as Mak's waist, and it slipped through the vines that draped the entrance.

Now almost completely blind, Mak followed. He hadn't expected the steeply sloped floor beyond and lost his footing. He slid down a dry earth slope and crumpled into the wolf's flank. Mak tensed as the animal gave a murmur, but not a growl. Then he felt it moving, getting comfortable on the floor. Its warm body pressed against him, feeling like a smelly, damp, but very comfortable fluffy blanket.

Gradually Mak felt himself relax as he realized that the animal was comforting him, keeping him warm. He stared into the darkness, which was now complete.

The slow rise and fall of the wolf's chest was soothing, and he heard a gentle whimpering indicating she was asleep. And as all his tension at last began to leach from him, Mak was hit with a wave of fatigue that swept away both his trepidation and even the very insistent rumbling of his stomach.

And so he slept.

CHAPTER TWENTY-ONE

MAK'S EYES FLICKED OPEN the moment something wet and coarse ran across his face. He restrained every urge to panic—which was helped by the cute ball of fluff in front of him. A small wolf pup industriously licked his face while a second nuzzled around his feet.

Light streamed in from the sloping entrance, illuminating the small den. The earth was dry, and piles of brown leaves added to the primitive comfort level. Mak slowly sat up, so as not to scare his new companions. There was no sign of their mother.

Mak scratched the nearest pup behind the ears and it responded by tilting its head, demanding more.

"You like that?" He furiously scratched, much to the pup's delight. "I'll call you Little Itch."

The other pup licked Mak's foot, which, despite the throbbing pain on his soles, tickled him. "Hey! Cut that out! I wouldn't lick those feet in a million years." In response, the pup gave a single shrill bark. "Looks like I'll be calling you Little Yip."

Mak stretched—and banged his head on the low ceiling. "Ouch!"

The two pups finished licking him, then scrambled up the slope and nuzzled their way out through the vine-covered entrance.

"Hey, where are you going?"

On his hands and knees, Mak followed. He squinted as he emerged into the daylight and it took a few seconds for his eyes to adjust. He was not surprised to find it was still raining, although it had eased considerably overnight, and what clouds he could see through the canopy were lighter than the severe black ones he had become accustomed to.

He stretched, every bone in his body clicking as he did so. He slowly turned—and froze when he saw the wolf had silently appeared behind them. Clamped in her jaws was a young fawn almost as big as she was. She dragged it by the throat and dropped it in front of them.

The two pups moved closer, sniffing enthusiastically. Then they began to tear into the carcass. Their tiny paws ripped skin, the cute little mouths that had been licking him only moments before were soon stained with blood, as needle-sharp tiny teeth tore into the deer.

Mak couldn't pull his gaze away. Within moments this serene fairy-tale scene had transformed into a horror story, as bright red internal organs were exposed and the pups sank their fangs into them. Despite the gore, Mak's stomach rumbled harder than ever. The metallic scent of blood seemed almost welcoming and, to the astonishment of the civilized voice nagging at the back of his head, Mak edged closer to the kill as Itch and Yip tore into the flesh with satisfied growls.

Blood oozed from a tender chunk of dark flesh that looked like a slab of uncooked liver he'd once seen in a butcher's tray . . . And the aroma of fresh meat . . . he hadn't smelled anything like it for what seemed like ages, though it was probably only a few days.

He edged even closer, unable to look away. As if sensing his reluctance, the wolf nudged the corpse toward Mak. Yip and Itch had had their fill and were now licking the blood from their paws.

With a shaking hand, Mak reached out and touched a glistening internal organ. It was still warm.

Survival of the fittest: It was a phrase that he'd heard before—but outside the comforts of London, out here in the middle of nowhere, it made sense. If he didn't eat, he would die. Taking a deep breath, he pulled at the organ. Blood oozed across his hands, making the meat difficult to grip. Whatever the organ was, it remained steadfastly attached to the rest of the deer, so all he succeeded in doing was dragging its body closer.

With great reluctance, Mak moved onto his knees and leaned forward, shoving his head closer to the carcass. The smell was powerful, although still not as sickening as Mak had anticipated.

Closing his eyes, he slipped a small section of the flesh into his mouth and bit down. It was surprisingly tough to chew through and he was forced to tear at it. His body's gag reflex kicked in—but with an empty stomach he had nothing to throw up.

He forced the mouthful down.

It didn't taste too bad. He doubted it would be on the menu of any burger bar soon, but . . .

He took another, bigger mouthful, shaking his head this way and that to tear the meat. Before he knew it, his hunger had driven him to devour the entire lump of meat in his hand. He sat back on his haunches and stared at his bloodied fingers. Even the thick dirt under his nails was tinged red. He took stock of what he had just done and was impressed and repulsed in equal measure. Once more that nagging voice at the back of his mind: His dad wouldn't call him weak now, would he?

Mak let out a burp so loud a pair of birds watching from the branch above took flight in a blaze of blue and orange. Mak burst into laughter. Tears streamed down his face and he rolled on the ground, crying and laughing with mounting hysteria as the desperation of his circumstances became clear.

When he eventually calmed down, he noticed that the mother wolf had finished off the remains of the deer and was now leading her pups off into the forest.

"Hey! Wait for me!"

Mak wiped his bloodied hands in the dirt and quickly followed. As he did so, he noticed a large mushroom, the same type he had found the night before. This one had several gnawed teeth marks in it, indicating *something* had found it edible. He tore a piece of fungus and sniffed it. It smelled like dirt. He put it into his mouth and chewed. He couldn't identify the taste but was surprised by the hint of nut. It absorbed the taste of blood in his mouth. Feeling refreshed, he bounded after the wolf pack.

CHAPTER TWENTY-TWO

FROM AFAR, the boulder was like a scar in the lush jungle. Mak had mistaken the huge smooth brown boulders for enormous elephants when Mother Wolf had first led them here.

The hill didn't rise very high, enclosed as it was by trees, but the broad sandstone rocks kept the foliage at bay for several hundred feet, allowing a burbling stream to cut through in an almost straight line before it vanished into the forest.

The wolves sat on the banks, tails in the air as they took turns drinking the water. Mak was unsure what to do, knowing that drinking contaminated water was a potential killer. Still, this looked as clear as glass and was fast running. He considered straining the water through his sock, but thought that would probably make it even worse. The thought at least made him smile.

With no other choice, he joined the wolves and gulped the cool liquid before splashing it across his face to cool himself down. It was only then that he realized the rain had finally stopped and the sky above was now a deep azure blue.

Slowly, the cubs lay down in the sunlight.

Mak also found a broad boulder to lie on and spread himself out as wide as he could. Basking with his eyes closed, he could almost feel his clothes drying off, so he didn't move, save only to dry his back, for what seemed like hours.

The wolves stayed close, the mother keeping a watchful eye on both the pups and Mak. It was deceptively easy to feel safe in that moment, but Mak's darker thoughts swiftly intruded.

No search party . . .

They think you're dead . . .

The voice in his head was his own, but it spoke with such conviction that Mak could easily believe he was being told cold hard facts.

"NO!" he bellowed to the sky—startling Itch and Yip, who had been playfully squabbling on the bank. He had watched plenty of television shows about people being lost, even sometimes being forced to drink their own urine to survive. Well, he wasn't *that* desperate, at least not yet, and he had no intention of giving up. Somehow he felt that was what would determine whether he lived or died. Never give up.

CHAPTER TWENTY-THREE

"Where am I?" Mak said to himself. Speaking the words aloud seemed to fend off the nagging voice that wanted him to admit defeat.

He looked around. The clearing he was in was wide, but from the air it probably still looked like a dot. If he could send smoke signals . . . but that would mean lighting a fire. He put that idea to the back of his mind.

Instead, maybe he needed to assess the lay of the land.

He stood up, wincing the moment his feet took his weight. He sat back down on the warm rocks and examined his feet. They looked gruesome, resembling something that belonged buried in the pages of a medical textbook.

He checked his sneaker. Putting it back on wouldn't

work. One wasn't enough, and hopping through the jungle would probably kill him. Besides, the thick sole had worn away so that it was almost smooth, which explained why he'd been slipping everywhere before.

Then a thought struck him.

He took out the plastic spoon and, with the help of a thin stone, carefully split it down the middle, creating a jagged knife-edge. He ran his finger along it; it wasn't too sharp, but he hoped it would do the trick. Unlacing the sneaker, he then set about sawing horizontally through its rubber sole. It was tricky, but once he'd prized the sole off the shoe, he managed to slice it vertically into two thinner halves. As he peeled them apart he noticed that his hack-job had also created an uneven surface on both parts and they now had a better grip than before.

He used his new spoon-knife to slice through the shoelace, then used both lace halves to bind the new soles to his feet. They slipped around a little, but after some readjustment and feeding the lace between his toes, they at least offered some protection.

The wolves didn't seem at all interested in his exploits, so he clambered up the steepest boulder he could find, the rubber on his now-protected feet doing a grand job of stopping him from slipping off.

Mak felt like a true adventurer as he scaled the top of the highest boulder, but even from this lofty perch all he could see were the tops of yet more trees.

He needed to get higher.

Behind him a huge tree grew from the top of Boulder Hill. Massive ancient roots had punctured through gaps in the stone and now resembled a gnarled claw at the base of the tree.

Mak couldn't help but give the tree a personality—and it wasn't a nice one. In his imagination it was a cranky old man, the boughs angled over the boulders in an arthritic stoop. The lower twisting limbs occasionally moved in the gentle breeze, giving the impression it was waving thousands of tiny fists at him, warning Mak not to approach.

It felt as though the tree was doing all it could to dissuade him from climbing it, and Mak had no wish to argue.

CHAPTER TWENTY-FOUR

SO IT WAS THAT MAK fell into a routine. Each night he would retire to the wolves' den and snuggle up to Mother Wolf, more for safety than warmth.

Each morning a fresh new kill was presented to the cubs, and Mak waited his turn to eat. It became easier each time, although when the wolf mother presented them with a porcupine, Mak had to be especially careful not to stab himself on the ferocious quills. He even removed two from the she-wolf's side when it was clear she couldn't reach them herself. Then they would head to Boulder Hill to drink and frolic in the sun. Mak found more fungi and even a few nuts that kept his stomach full.

He made sure that he kept the mother, Yip, and Itch amused with his spinning-coin trick, and even teased them by bouncing the light off the shiny surface, causing the pups to run in circles chasing the reflected dot on the floor. They would leap onto the beam like hunters, then look around in confusion when they discovered the spot of light had escaped from under their paws.

It kept Mak amused.

It was a form of contentment, but each day he would study the sky, waiting for the first sign of a rescue plane and listening intently for the distant dull tone of an aircraft.

And each day they failed to arrive.

By possibly the fourth day a black mood had descended on Mak, and he refused to eat the unidentifiable critter presented to them. Help was not coming. That much was clear. The whispering voices, taunting him as to whether his parents were alive, had even changed tack, pointing out that this was the place Mak would die.

He knew he couldn't stay still any longer, which meant he would have to find his own way home. His attention increasingly turned to the crooked tree standing sentinel over the hill. As ever, the branches waved menacingly to put him off climbing, but Mak knew he must.

The trunk itself was as broad as his bedroom back home, and the craggy bark offered many footholds. In addition the tree tilted at a gentle angle over the edge of the boulder, offering a relatively easy climb.

Mak hadn't climbed a tree for years—and even then he had a clear memory of falling out and his dad shouting at him. But it offered the best view around, and if from there he could see signs of the camp, or even the river, then he would have hope.

A pep talk was in order. "You can do this, Mak!"

Just don't fall and break your neck, added the unwelcome voice of his father.

The first section of the tree was surprisingly easy. The crooked roots, which at first had seemed so imposing, allowed Mak to make short work of scrambling up the trunk. The crooked slender branches that had previously warned him away, now proved to be useful anchor points to pull himself upward.

Mak was surprised how his positive attitude had transformed the seemingly hostile obstacle into a more manageable challenge. True to his name, Yip circled the bottom of the tree, giving gruff barks of encouragement.

Mak reached the first broad branch with ease and sat straddled on it to catch his breath. Even from here he could see farther, although the vista was not encouraging—just more trees to the horizon. But Mak refused to be discouraged.

He needed to climb higher.

CHAPTER TWENTY-FIVE

A QUICK GLANCE BELOW to check on Yip proved to be a mistake. Even though Mak was only a quarter of the way up the tree, the drop yawned below him, threatening certain death if he took a misstep.

He felt his legs quiver, as if the strength had leaked out of them like air from a balloon. He closed his eyes—another mistake that caused him to wobble on the branch.

He opened them again and fixed his gaze on his destination above, hidden beyond the countless twisted lower limbs of the tree.

"You can do this," he said in a low voice.

The next stage of the climb was slower as the number of branches increased. Now he had to wend his way through them, hauling himself from one to another until his arms trembled from the exertion.

One thing was certain, the branches were becoming thinner. As he shoved his way higher they whipped at his face, leaving stinging marks across any exposed skin. His hand reached for a stem paler than the others—and it snapped under his weight.

Mak dropped a couple of feet onto a sturdier branch below. The impact was enough to wind him. One flailing hand caught another thin but strong branch, and he steadied himself.

His heart pounded as he imagined dropping like a pinball against the branches before his body snapped on the rocks below. He lay there for several moments before he realized he was still clutching the fragment of broken wood in his hand. It was dead, and parched so badly that it almost crumbled in his hand. He noticed the bark had been stripped clean and black marks stained the wood itself.

He twisted his head so he could see upward. To his surprise he had almost reached the top of the tree. He climbed steadily up the last several feet.

From the ground he hadn't seen that the tip of the tree was scorched black, from a lightning strike, he guessed. Being one of the tallest points in the jungle, it had suffered a direct hit, and relentless monsoon winds had probably forced the tree to the angle it now grew.

Suddenly Mak felt almost sorry for the mighty tree. No longer did he see it as a grouchy, bent old man, but as a resilient warrior determined to grow no matter what Mother Nature threw at it. He was no longer afraid of it, or the drop below.

Mak stood and took a deep breath as he balanced himself. The crown of the tree had long, slender branches that offered views in every direction as he hopped from one to another, a hand resting against the damaged trunk for support.

In one direction Mak could see the jungle steadily rising, and the peaks of jagged mountains beyond. He didn't recall any mountains on the helicopter flight into the jungle, so he reasoned that was not the way to go.

He shifted position and peered across the rest of the jungle. All hope of seeing a sweeping river cutting through the landscape was dashed. He was certain there was one there—but the view of it was blocked by the jungle canopy stretching toward the shimmering haze of the horizon.

"HELLO?" he yelled as loudly as he could. "HEEELLLOOO!"

Nothing stirred. Mak hadn't expected an answer, but the lack of one still made his heart sink. If he was going to walk out of this in one piece he needed to take control. Logic told him that the jungle had to end eventually. He recalled the pilot saying they were traveling northeast into the jungle, which meant they had traveled from the southwest. Which way was that?

The sun was overhead; then again it usually was. However, he could see from his position the direction in which it rose and sank. He drew an imaginary line between the two. It wasn't accurate, but it was enough for him to turn and face southwest-ish.

It looked just like every other patch of jungle, offering not a single landmark that would provide a useful navigation reference. Still, it was a direction, and even a vague destination offered the promise of hope.

With this sliver of optimism in his back pocket, Mak began the climb down. The descent proved much easier, although different muscles from the ones he had used going up now began to ache. He stopped for a rest on a wide branch and allowed his legs to dangle off the edge as he took in the view.

It was several moments before he realized that he wasn't alone on the branch.

CHAPTER TWENTY-SIX

MAK FROZE as the snake slowly uncoiled from the leaves.

Already half of its body was extended, and Mak judged the snake was longer than he was tall. The serpent's belly was white, its dark upper surface marked with white dots along the spine and white bands down the side. Its beady black eyes were fixed on Mak, its tongue flicking as it sensed the air.

It was a krait, one of the deadliest snakes in India. Mak didn't know the name, but he knew from the delta-shaped head that it was venomous. Mak reflexively scrabbled backward along the branch—which immediately gave way under his weight.

The crack of wood was so loud, it vibrated through his body. As Mak dropped, branches whipped his face so hard he tasted blood. The fall was short, his path blocked by a firm wooden bough that knocked the breath from his lungs. However, it was a brief respite as this branch gave way in turn—but not before Mak saw the broken spur from above lance toward his head, the writhing krait still attached to it.

Mak's shoulders struck another tree limb, sending him tumbling sideways—a move that probably saved his life as another jagged bough whooshed past his head, nicking his ear. The sound of snapping branches was incredible. He closed his eyes to protect them as shorter twigs lashed him as he fell.

He felt something warm and smooth slide across his leg—but it was gone in a moment.

Mak threw his arms over his head as smaller branches cascaded over him, painfully rebounding. Then, as suddenly as it began, the nightmare tumble was over.

All was still again.

Mak opened his eyes and was surprised to discover he was still in the tree. Hurt, but still sitting upright, he expected he would be heavily bruised after this misadventure. The last branch of the tree had saved him from crashing onto the boulders below—and sustaining a serious injury. He checked his stinging arms, which were covered in a fine network of thin scratches but thankfully nothing too deep.

Then he remembered the snake.

He tensed as he looked around, but could see no sign of it. He gingerly pulled the legs of his dirty jeans up. He had felt the snake move across him and dreaded seeing a puncture wound from its fangs—but there was nothing there.

Mak expelled a long breath. He had escaped near death twice in a single moment—he *had* to be more careful.

With no desire to hang around in the tree, Mak carefully made his way back down to the boulders where Yip and Itch were playing tug-of-war with one of the many branches that had dropped, oblivious to his near-death experience.

He bathed his cuts in the stream and thought about the journey ahead. Already it seemed impossible. His frustration grew.

"Why is it so difficult to find a river?" he bellowed, watching as the red taint of his blood was quickly swept downstream.

Downstream.

It was as if a veil of doubt and despair had been blocking the logical thoughts from his mind.

Of course the stream would link to the river eventually—all he had to do was follow it! He began to chuckle, amazed by his own stupidity. Attracted by the laughter, the two pups came over and nuzzled him inquisitively. Mak scratched their heads and they curled up close to him. He lay back and stared at the sky. It was too late to make a move now, but at first light he would set out and follow the stream.

CHAPTER TWENTY-SEVEN

THAT NIGHT'S SLEEP was the best Mak could remember, despite his damaged body. The moment they had entered the den he had fallen into a deep slumber, all dreams obliterated by exhaustion.

When he awoke, it was morning, and the wolves were not there.

He scrambled outside into the bright sunlight, every movement finding a new, painful bruise on his body. He found the pack feeding on something he couldn't identify, as the cubs had torn it to shreds. Still, he helped himself to whatever pieces were left, after carefully cleaning out the thick black gunk that had formed under his fingernails. There was no point in poisoning himself now that he had a plan for escape!

Only after he'd eaten did he realize this was the

first time he hadn't felt disgust at eating raw meat. He still didn't find it pleasant, but his mother had certainly dished up worse meals.

As usual he followed the wolves to Boulder Hill and drank, splashing reviving water across his face. The skies were clear and the heat stronger than ever when he announced his plans to his adoptive family.

"I have to find my parents. My human ones," he added when the wolves looked inquisitively at him. He pointed downstream, but their gaze just fell to his finger—not the direction. "I'm following the stream to the river. That's where I came from. Will you come with me?"

Of course he didn't expect an answer, so he began walking along the bank to where the stream vanished into the trees. He issued a series of short whistles in what he assumed was the international canine language, then patted his leg for good measure.

"Come on, guys."

The wolves watched him, amused, but whatever entertainment value Mak held for them was short-lived—a dragonfly the size of his hand then set down across the stream. The pups darted into action and chased it. Only Mother Wolf held Mak's gaze. Emotion unexpectedly washed over him.

"Thanks for watching over me," he said, his voice cracking. He dipped his head toward her in respect. He didn't know if it would mean anything to the animal, but it felt like the right thing to do. His venture ahead suddenly seemed a lot less appealing without the wolves, compared to the ease of staying put—but go he must.

Mak wiped a tear from his eye, and stepped forward into the jungle.

MAK MARCHED DETERMINEDLY along the streambed as it weaved along the jungle floor, his makeshift sandals protecting his feet from the rocks beneath. The canopy above appeared to close up, obscuring any view of the sky, and with it the humidity increased, until Mak felt he was being boiled alive.

The banks of the stream became steeper, bordered by plants so tangled and thick that Mak had no hope of breaking through them without a machete. Instead he was forced to wade through the water, which was becoming noticeably deeper as he pressed on. From shin-deep to waist-deep, Mak had no choice but to continue through, thankful that his feet were protected from some of the sharper stones he stumbled across.

Several times the stream flowed over an abrupt edge, forming little waterfalls no taller than Mak. Even these became problems as the wet moss clinging to the rocks was as slick as ice, and Mak constantly lost his footing and fell into the water.

It was never more than chest-deep, yet Mak was

now much more concerned about slipping and breaking a bone—a danger he had narrowly avoided in his fall from the tree and one that he suspected would prevent him from ever getting out of the jungle alive.

CHAPTER TWENTY-EIGHT

JUDGING TIME by his rumbling stomach, Mak gauged it was past midday when he was finally forced out of the water. The current in the stream was picking up and had tugged at his feet, making each step more dangerous than the last. He climbed up the steep river-bank to rest and was greeted with the sight of more edible fungi and several green fruits a little larger than his fist, temptingly hanging from a branch.

He plucked the fruit and sniffed it. To Mak the fruit smelled like everything else around him.

Digging his fingers into the flesh, he tore the husk in half and was greeted with a pungent and familiar smell: mango! He gorged himself on several fruit, thankful for a taste other than fungi and raw meat. The sticky juice covered his face and fingers, but he didn't care. With a full belly and the warm air, it was tempting to fall asleep, but Mak rallied himself. Escape lay onward.

Energized, Mak stuffed several mangoes in his lone sock, tied it to a belt-loop on his jeans, and set off again.

His progress was slowed considerably by yet more thick tree roots lining the bank, but the stream itself was becoming wider, carving a deeper trough through the floor. Mak struggled on until, without warning, the trees suddenly stopped and he stepped out onto a muddy riverbank.

The stream he had been following now flowed into a broad river. Mak's heart sang as he looked out across the slow-moving brown water—he had found his river!

Looking in both directions, he could see the river curved away, offering nothing more than a wall of distant trees and no hint of what lay beyond. Not that that mattered; he could see very clearly which way the water flowed and knew he had to head back downstream to get to the village.

How hard could that be?

AFTER AN EXHAUSTING WALK DOWNSTREAM, Mak saw that the river slowly turned to the left, and with it his side of the bank sliced through vertical rock. Following it from the shore was going to be problematic if not impossible.

"I need a raft," he said to a colorful kingfisher perched on a fallen log. It regarded him for a moment—then darted into the water, flying out with a flash of silver caught between its beak.

"Wood floats," he reasoned. "And there's plenty of it around!"

Mak lay five logs, a little longer than his body, down one way in the mud, then, selecting three shorter ones, he braced his raft horizontally. He could already see the shape of the vessel that would carry him to safety.

After much searching he found a thin stone with a sharp edge, which he used to hack off stray branches from his logs. And the final results were worth it.

Now all he had to do was bind it all together. He shimmied up several nearby trees and used his improvised plastic knife to saw through some dangling vines. They proved to be ideal rope with which he could bind the raft together.

After several hours Mak's ship was complete, topped off with a broad length of rotted tree that still retained a gentle curve, which he would employ as a primitive paddle.

Feeling rather of proud of himself, Mak tilted his head to the sky and bellowed: "I AM MASTER OF THE JUNGLE!" Then almost at once, Mak felt a bit embarrassed and looked around to make sure no one was watching.

Several birds had taken flight, but nothing else had stirred. It was as if the jungle was holding its breath, waiting to see Mak's next move.

He lifted up one side of the raft and dragged it toward the water. It weighed a little more than he'd anticipated. Placing the paddle onboard, he dropped the raft's leading edge into the water with a splash.

"I name this ship *HMS Escape!*"

He pushed the raft into the water—but it refused to move, the majority of it stuck in the mud. With more grunting, he dragged the raft farther into the river, releasing it when he was waist-deep. He had expected it to float proudly—instead it dipped alarmingly beneath the surface. Mak panicked—*What have I done wrong?*

CHAPTER TWENTY-NINE

THE RAFT FLOATED—sort of—though it was a full inch beneath the water. But the current had already begun to take it out into the deeper part of the river.

The water's tannin-brown color obscured any view of what was lurking beneath, and Mak's confidence was rapidly evaporating.

He tried to climb aboard, but every time he put weight on the raft it would sink lower while the opposite end seesawed out from the water. His carry-sock containing the mangoes and spoon-knife fell away as Mak frantically gripped the edge of the raft so that his feet cleared the bottom of the river. Now he was at the mercy of the current and found himself being pulled farther away from the shore.

Desperately, Mak lunged to clamber onto the raft once again. The top half of his body made it, his fingers grasping for purchase between the gaps in the slippery logs. He heaved himself aboard, but the opposite side of the raft rose out of the water like a wind-surfer's sail. His paddle slipped off, clocking him with a painful blow across the shin.

Mak tried to redistribute his weight in order to force the raft back into the water. Instead a crack shuddered across the raft as the vine-rope binding suddenly tore. He opened his mouth to scream—but instead gulped down brown water as the raft flipped over completely. The now-unbound logs scattered, one cracking him on the shoulder and forcing him underwater.

He swung his arms and legs but felt nothing but pain as the spars of his raft hit him one after the other—shoving him lower into the water.

He had escaped drowning in the river once before, and a nagging voice in his head told him he had been a fool to challenge it again. This was how he was going to die, and it was all his own fault.

Something then yanked his shoulder and he felt himself being pulled sideways. He wanted to lash out to free himself but found his movements were sluggish and weak. Just as he was about to accept his fate, he was dragged into the shallows of the river. He rolled over and coughed up the water in his lungs—then gasped for air, all the while muttering to his savior, "Thank you, thank you . . ."

Sucking in a deep breath, he rolled over and was surprised to see . . . Mother Wolf. The magnificent animal shook her fur dry, then circled around and licked Mak's face until he giggled.

"Stop it! That tickles!"

He couldn't stop himself from clambering to his knees and hugging the wild creature. The wolf accepted it for a few moments before shucking him loose and walking proudly off to check on Yip and Itch, who had been watching from the safety of a rock.

Mak wondered if they had been watching him all day, and was thankful if they had. Yet again he owed his life to these unlikely guardians.

He turned his attention back to the river. Only two of the spars he'd used for the raft were visible as they slowly spiraled downstream on their path to civilization, a path he had no hope of navigating. As he studied the river, he tried to recall anything familiar about the banks on either side.

Admittedly one tree looked very much like another, and he recalled their captain had diverted them from one river into a tributary at least twice . . .

For the first time it dawned on him that this might not even be the *right* river.

Exhausted and hopeless, he lay on his back to preserve what little strength he had left. His plans were now in tatters.

CHAPTER THIRTY

MAK'S DETOUR to the river had spurred Mother Wolf to leave the den behind and travel. As if sensing Mak's desire, they headed downstream, keeping as close to the river as possible.

Mak kept close to the pack—and time passed. At times they moved to higher ground and had no view of the river for days at a time.

And then the rain came.

Mak lost track of time. Of place. The relentless rain made it impossible for Mak to see where they were going half the time—but it didn't stop them from moving. Never pausing for long, with Mak's eyes fixed on the ground ahead, his mind focused on just the next step to keep him going.

With all the traveling, the family had to find

new places to sleep, which was not an easy task. Sometimes they were lucky to find rock ledges and overhangs that protected them from the driving rain; other times they could find refuge only under over-hanging boughs.

This forced Mak and the pups to lay close to Mother Wolf. Still Mak was soaked to the bone each night, despite trying to dry himself off with moss or even in dry patches of dirt. He'd heard about *trench foot* be-fore in a history lesson and was worried he would get it if it kept raining like this.

The thought that a history lesson might actually be responsible for helping save his life made him smile . . .

The choice of food became leaner. One morning Mak was greeted with the gift of a large game bird after the pups had finished with it. It was nothing more than a mass of feathers and bone and he just couldn't bring himself to chew on those. Instead, Mak opted to bite into an unfamiliar fruit he'd found, but its sharp taste made him sick almost instantly. His illness lasted the whole day and left him straggling behind the wolves as they picked their way along the river.

WITH THE CONSTANT RAIN, pains in his stomach, no clear plan, and now the darkness of yet another night closing in on them, Mak felt increasing despair. His nights had become riddled with vivid dreams depicting his mother and father clinging to a log as the river swelled around them.

Everything appeared in his mind's eye with high-definition clarity yet moved with agonizing slowness.

He watched, frozen, before reaching for his parents as they sank beneath the waves. Each night he would wake with a start; and each subsequent night the dream came back with a vengeance, and he would attempt to save them again . . . and again . . . and again . . .

Only the constant company of the wolves kept Mak going. Even when they had been forced to dig in the dirt to unearth glistening brown grubs that they gobbled down, Mak went along with them. He held a writhing larva between his thumb and forefinger and drew it closer for inspection.

Dirt stuck to its glistening flank, its fat, swollen body larger than his thumb. Closing his eyes, Mak held the grub in his mouth, careful that it didn't touch his tongue—he had no desire to taste it. He tilted his head back, counted to three, and dropped it down his throat.

He swore he could feel it wriggling all the way down. However, he was surprised by the wood-like aftertaste. It was far more pleasant than he had any reason to believe it would be. It was amazing what you could eat when you had to, Mak thought.

THE DAYS PASSED, along with the miles, as Mak continued down the river. He now knew for sure that this was not the same river that had swallowed him. He really had lost track of time—had weeks passed? How could he tell? Only by the fact that the dark images of his family had begun to fade, replaced by nothing more than deep, dreamless slumber.

He was becoming the jungle.

CHAPTER THIRTY-ONE

IT WAS NO LONGER RAINING when the banks changed from mud to sand and the river began to turn in sharp loops. It was while cutting across the golden sands of one such beach that Mak stopped in his tracks.

The sand was rutted with a series of paw prints that led from the trees to the water's edge. Mak crouched to inspect them and felt a shiver of recognition—they were big-cat prints. The claw marks clearly visible in the sand were just as he'd seen before, except this time the experience revealed more information to him.

There was no rainwater in the prints, and the sand kicked up around them was still relatively dry, meaning they had been created recently, perhaps even in the past hour. Mak looked around in alarm—could the creature still be around? He noticed the wolves stood alert, ears pivoted toward the trees.

Mak tensed. Some primeval instinct was telling him there was danger close by, not to hang around, but he wanted to know more. He slowly crawled on his hands and knees toward the water, following the prints. He could even see where the cat had crouched to drink, its long tail brushing ripples in the sand.

Curiously the prints here were deeper and led away at a sharp angle, back into the trees. As if it had run at speed chasing something . . . or had been chased.

The thought was barely formed when the water in front of him exploded and the world slowed.

Jagged teeth framed a set of jaws that extended from the water—aimed straight for him. Mak sprang from his crouch, darting sideways in a move that saved his life. He felt a rush of air as the powerful jaws slammed shut with a single heavy thud.

He rolled over onto his shoulder and was up on his feet again. A quick glance behind him revealed the mighty bulk of a crocodile as it hauled itself from the river. Water glistened on its flanks as the beast struggled to change direction toward him.

Mak didn't even think. He sprinted toward the trees, following the path of the big cat, which had no doubt endured the same attack. The wolves were ahead, growling and barking furiously—but as soon as Mak caught up with them they turned and fled into the trees.

His arms pumped hard as he ran, springing over roots and ducking under branches without thought. He finally stopped when Mother Wolf did, and they turned back to see the enormous reptile had stopped pursuing them halfway along the beach and had instead slumped on the sand to bask.

Mak doubled over to catch his breath and looked sidelong at the wolves.

"Maybe we should keep away from the water for a bit?"

As if in understanding, Mother Wolf continued deeper into the forest. They followed a foraging trail that made progress for the rest of the day easier. Mak couldn't help but notice Mother Wolf was now stopping more frequently, ears pricked for unwelcome sounds in the breeze and nose on alert for any scent that shouldn't be there.

He recalled the fresh paw prints in the sand, and he too scanned the trees for any predators that might be stalking them.

The close encounter with the crocodile had shaken him. Even with a wolf pack by his side, the jungle was dangerous. He was thankful for the safety the wolves afforded him and wondered if Mother Wolf was thinking the same: that there was safety in numbers.

CHAPTER THIRTY-TWO

ANOTHER COUPLE OF DAYS passed without further incident, and Mak was relieved when Mother Wolf returned with larger prey once again: a hog that offered plenty of food for the hungry.

By now Mak was even joining the pups while they ate rather than waiting for their leftovers. He'd studied what parts of the innards the pups went for first, so he was able to select the most nutritious meat—such as the liver—and avoid the sickening stench of the pig's burst stomach.

One day they entered a wide glade that offered a picturesque waterfall pouring from a rock face some two stories high. The water cut through the jungle to join the main river, which they had not returned to for days, although Mak kept seeing it through the occasional gaps in the trees.

Without the ever-present tree coverage, the rain fell harder on him. It hadn't stopped for over a week, and Mak was beginning to forget what it felt like to be dry. He left the wolves to drink from the stream while he set off to explore the clearing.

It was only about the size of a soccer field, but as he moved away from the waterfall his new position allowed him to see a little over the trees.

The rock from which the waterfall flowed was just the base of a sharp incline that teetered steadily upward. Mak glimpsed distant mountain peaks and was puzzled; the only mountains he had seen lay in the opposite direction from the one he wished to get to . . . With a sinking heart he realized that by following the river they had circled around in completely the wrong direction.

He expected to feel despair and defeat, but to his surprise he felt nothing. The old Mak would have been yelling to the heavens at the unfairness of it all.

Not now. He felt calmer. There was no point in wasting energy shouting and ranting; it wouldn't change a thing. At least he was still alive, and while he was alive he had the power to change things.

His senses were more attuned to the environment now. He closed his eyes and the sounds of the jungle amplified. The patter of rain on the leaves around him; the gentle grunts from Itch and Yip; the dull throb of the waterfall . . . and something else.

He angled his head, cupping his hands behind his ears, which had the effect of raising the jungle's volume switch. There was a constant noise coming from the direction of the river. Curious, Mak headed toward the tree line, and the sound got louder. Machinery possibly? And if there was machinery . . .

"People . . ." He gasped excitedly.

He took off through the trees at a run, hopping over boulders and vaulting across fallen logs. The weeks had certainly toned him up from the couch potato he had been back in London, and he felt empowered by it. Ahead he could see smoke, and the noise grew louder with every step.

The ground before him suddenly vanished, and Mak grabbed a tree to stop himself from plummeting over a precipice that suddenly yawned before him. It hadn't been machinery, but the rumbling of an enormous crescent-shaped waterfall that blocked any further progress downstream.

The smoke was a veil of mist kicked up by the falls, obscuring the view across the water at the bottom. The riverbank he stood on was the lip of a gorge that dropped straight into the mist below.

The earth shook beneath his feet. At first he took it to be the power of the falls, but it was getting stronger.

Then he heard the howl of Mother Wolf—the hairs on the back of his neck prickled instantly and he sprinted back toward the clearing.

With each step the air seemed to reverberate with the mighty rumble. Mak burst into the clearing to see the wolves facing toward the mountains, howling in alarm.

Then he saw why.

CHAPTER THIRTY-THREE

THE TOPS OF THE TREES swayed and cracked as if something enormous was ploughing its way through the jungle toward them. The clearing's pleasant little waterfall suddenly became a torrent, as some unseen force pushed the water before it. Then the water turned black, and rocks, dirt, and broken trees were hurled over the edge.

A second later a wall of churning mud and water crashed through the forest—the spearhead of a mighty flash flood. There had been a massive landslide upstream, as part of the distant mountain had finally given way under the relentless monsoon rains.

Mother Wolf stood across the other side of the clearing as the flash flood tore between her and Mak faster than he could run. Mak saw Itch race to his mother's side, but for some reason Mother Wolf wasn't fleeing. Then Mak saw why . . .

Yip had become separated, and was on Mak's side of the approaching divide. If he ran for his mother the young pup would undoubtedly be crushed, yet that was exactly what he was trying to do.

Mak yelled as he raced toward the pup. "YIP! NO!"

The little wolf hesitated on hearing Mak's voice— but it stood no chance of avoiding the side of the mountain bearing down on it. Broken tree logs, complete with roots, were surging toward the defenseless animal.

Mak gritted his teeth and ran as hard as he could. He made it to the terrified pup just before the landslide did, and scooped it up in his arms. Looking around he realized that all he had done was risk getting them both killed.

No. He'd come too far for that. This wasn't just about survival anymore; this was Mak versus the jungle—and he had no intention of losing.

He hurled Yip toward his mother. The young pup landed in a tumble, but was instantly on its feet and running for the safety of the trees with his family. Mak saw Mother Wolf cast one look behind before the maelstrom was upon him.

Mak ducked to the side as a huge tree root thundered past. He leaped onto the fallen tree just as the mud was about to sweep him off his feet. With remarkable balance he didn't know he possessed, Mak remained crouching on the log as it hurtled him across the clearing.

Behind him, with a noise like the earth splitting open, came a churning wave of stone, mud, and mangled trees. All Mak could do was keep his balance, even though he knew what lay ahead—the gorge.

He gripped the tree root, holding on for dear life—and then he was suddenly soaring through the air.

The constant roar of the flash flood was almost deafening—but Mak could still feel it through every bone in his body. Even his teeth vibrated together.

With one hand clutching a thick branch, the other outstretched to control his balance, Mak half-surfed the torrent, even as he was pitched across the gorge.

The shaking stopped for a moment as the entire tree took to the air.

Mak clung on.

A constant spray of mud was kicked into his face and Mak was forced to bury his head between his arms as stones and pebbles painfully bounced off his body.

Then suddenly it was over. The roaring subsided, and his tree stump rolled to a stop, caught in between two boulders on the high-sided banks of the river. Mak's arms were so stiffly wrapped around it that they felt locked in place and it was painful to straighten them. Somewhere along the ride he had lost his sandals, and his bare toes wriggled in the mud.

Behind him the flash flood of mud and debris had carved a clear scar through the jungle, with trees smashed down like matchsticks and replaced with a highway of mud and stone.

He looked back to where he thought he had come from. The distant mountains were just visible, but definitely smaller.

Where the trees had been uprooted Mak could see more of the sky, and he was relieved to see glimpses of blue. The monsoon rains were once again receding. The brief glimmer of the sun also gave him the chance to judge in which direction he had been carried. South-ish was the best he could gauge.

Ahead, the jungle continued in an almost-solid wall of trees.

Then, as if the sky had been holding its breath, the rain began to patter down once more.

There was no sign of the wolves.

He howled as loudly as he could, hoping to hear Mother Wolf's reply, but nothing came. His initial worries gave way to hope as he recalled how he had thrown Yip to safety and the wolves had fled into the trees. He knew how fast they could move and was certain Mother Wolf would have led her family to safety.

But now what should he do? Return and find them? Would they attempt to come to him?

It was easy enough to believe the wolves behaved like humans, but Mak knew, despite their welcoming him as one of their own, they were still wild animals. The death of one of her pups had probably caused the mother to take pity on him, and for that he was thankful. With a heavy heart the truth of the situation became apparent: He was once again on his own and salvation lay somewhere southwest-ish . . .

"Onward!" he whispered to himself. "Onward and forward. Keep going, Mak."

And with that, and a deep-rooted fear, he returned to the depths of the jungle.

CHAPTER THIRTY-FOUR

ALTHOUGH THE CANOPY above Mak's head usually sheltered him from most of the rain, he at last became convinced that the rains had stopped altogether.

Bright glimpses of sunlight began to filter through the leaves, and with it the humidity of the jungle floor gradually increased until it felt as if he were walking through a steam bath. The effect was complete with a mist that hugged the ground, making each step a little more difficult, now that he couldn't see what he was standing on.

The relative silence of the jungle after the landslide slowly gave way to a chorus of exotic-sounding birds. He caught glimpses of colorful shapes darting high above, and their songs were a welcome relief that bolstered Mak's spirits.

He walked for hours before it finally occurred

to him why he still wasn't hungry. His thoughts had been very much on taking the next step, but his hands were automatically snatching nuts and berries as he passed them. Without thinking, he was avoiding the ones he suspected to be poisonous, and he felt a moment of pride at what he had learned so far. What would his father think of him now?

As quickly as the thought surfaced, Mak pushed it away. He wasn't ready for anymore night terrors. He had accepted the fact that no search party was looking for him, and as for the fate of his parents . . . he just couldn't contemplate it. He sighed. He would surrender to the law of the jungle and hope fervently that it would see him—and his parents—safely home.

GRADUALLY THE SKY slipped into twilight, and Mak saw ripples of cloud bathed in magnificent orange hues that hinted at a spectacular sunset he couldn't quite see. He was just thinking about finding a safe place for the night when a throaty reverberation stopped him in his tracks.

The mist parted before him, revealing the face of a killer.

It was a panther. The unmistakable soft ebony fur was punctuated by a unique pattern of paler black markings. This one sported a tuft of fur on its chin, like a wise old beard. But it was the eyes—wide, yellow—that fixed unblinkingly on Mak.

Mak's heart beat so loudly he wondered if the cat could hear it. His legs twitched as the instinct to flee kicked in, but there was no doubt that the panther would catch him. The feline's muscular body was designed to do *exactly* that.

Long moments passed and the panther didn't break eye contact or stop the threatening growl. Nor did it strike.

Mak took an experimental step backward. Still the panther didn't move. Something was clearly wrong. That's when Mak spotted the blood on the creature's throat; not from the remains of a meal, but from where something had cut across its flesh.

Despite his fear, Mak crouched for a better look. There was a length of wire coiled around the cat's neck, probably left by a poacher—and just above it was a thick rubber collar, which had obviously saved the animal from strangulation. Mak's heart began to beat faster as he peered more closely at the collar. It looked familiar, and on top of it was a GPS tracker, exactly like the one Anil had shown him!

A link to civilization. Perhaps he could somehow use it to contact his family? He wished he'd paid more attention when Anil had shown him the other tracker. But the snare meant people too, and possibly closer by.

Mak could barely contain the surge of hope and excitement that washed over him.

The panther was in no position to attack him, so

Mak slowly turned around, intent on giving the creature a wide berth. As he circled through the trees he saw the magnificent cat's head follow him, and he began to feel its pain.

"But it's a killer," he muttered, forcing himself to look away.

Being strangled by a poacher's snare, added the voice in his head. *Which makes people killers too . . .*

Mak stopped and regarded the creature. It was longer than he was tall, and he could see the deep gouges its claws had made in the log as it struggled in pain.

What if the wolves had left you . . . ?

His empathy for the panther increased. Mak took a deep breath and slowly turned back toward the beast.

"If I help you, will you promise not to eat me?" Mak hoped the panther would sense his nonthreatening tone and words.

The panther made no such promise. Still, Mak took a few steps forward. The creature didn't move.

Then one step closer . . .

CHAPTER THIRTY-FIVE

MAK WAS JUST WITHIN STRIKING DISTANCE of those powerful claws and he couldn't keep his eyes off them. As if sensing his intentions, the panther laid its head flat on the log, stretching itself out as best it could. Its claws retracted into its paws and the grumbling noise shifted into a deep purring.

"This is so crazy . . ." Mak muttered as he drew closer to the panther's side. With a trembling hand he slowly extended it to the beast's flank and gave it a short, soft stroke. His fingers vibrated as the purring increased tempo.

"Easy, boy . . . girl . . ." Mak was in no position to tell. He edged slowly up to the panther's neck, his fingers tracing over the GPS tracker. He saw the faint green power LED was illuminated, broadcasting the animal's position.

If he could take that off too . . .

It was an impossible task while the snare was still around the animal's neck. Shaking, Mak took the long end of the snare that stretched up into the branches of the nearby tree and tugged it to free up some slack. He managed just a little, but with luck it would be enough to slip the noose off.

Taking a deep breath, Mak slowly maneuvered the wire around the panther's head. He brushed past an ear—causing the animal to suddenly flinch. Mak froze, expecting to have his hand bitten off at any second.

The panther settled back down. With agonizing slowness, Mak continued moving the snare around the cat's muzzle. His hand passed before its mouth, and he could feel the hot air expelled as the animal slowly breathed out.

Then the snare came free of the animal's neck in a single fluid movement. The very second it was removed the panther bounded forward.

Mak could feel the creature tense as it scrambled toward another tree, powerful claws gripping the trunk as it effortlessly hauled itself up to the nearest branch. There the animal lay flat and, in an awkward movement, began licking its own bloody neck.

Mak laughed out loud, delighted that the magnificent animal was once again free, and impressed by his own courage. He closed his eyes and ran his fingers through his hair in relief. When he opened his eyes again the panther had disappeared.

And with it the GPS tracker that could have connected him to the outside world.

CHAPTER THIRTY-SIX

NIGHT FELL QUICKLY, and with it Mak found refuge in the broad curving limb of a drooping tree. Off the ground he felt safe and relatively confident that the panther would not return to harm him. He sensed there was a connection between them now . . . and hoped that was not just wishful thinking.

The thinning branches overhead granted a view of a sky dusted with stars, more than he had ever seen before. The jungle's nightly choir struck up and, for the first time, Mak found it both comforting and soothing. He closed his eyes and absently toyed with the coil of wire he had taken from around the panther's neck. While he was not happy with the injuries it had caused to the noble animal, the thought of poachers—of human contact—so close by filled him with hope. Combined with the big cat's GPS collar, he felt that home was now closer than ever.

He could almost hear his sister's teasing voice, taste his mother's ravioli, the food he had missed the most. Even his father's constant complaints were beginning to seem appealing . . .

He opened his eyes and gasped. Instead of being pitch black, the jungle was alive with ghostly blue and green hues. Mak rubbed his eyes, but still the image remained. Fireflies zipped between flowers like shooting stars, and the plants themselves glowed with a pale blue bioluminescence triggered by the passing monsoon rains. It was beautiful, and Mak felt as if he was stuck in the warm embrace of a watercolor painting. His eyes drooped . . . and he fell into a dreamless sleep.

ANOTHER TWO DAYS PASSED in peace as Mak pressed on through the jungle, mindful to check his position against the sun at intervals. Without a watch he couldn't judge precisely which way he was going, but he began using the shadows cast by the sun to help guide him.

Planting a stick in the ground, he'd mark the position, then wait for maybe fifteen or thirty minutes, as best as he could judge, and then mark the new position of the sun. Standing between the two points, he *assumed* he was facing south.

The more he walked, the easier he found identifying the trees and bushes offering mangoes, berries, and nuts. Supplemented with the occasional chunk of fungus, this now formed his regular diet. He began to miss meat, even raw meat. And the thought of chocolate made his mouth water.

Other things became apparent. Moss carpeted rocks and trees wherever it could, although it tended to be thicker on the side away from the sun. There also tended to be more spiderwebs on the northward-facing side of the trunks. It was basic navigation, but it assured him he was going in the right direction.

SITTING ON A ROCK at the side of a clear stream, Mak watched the fat bodies of fish swim below him. On impulse he found a straight branch, rubbed one end against a rock until it was sharp, or at least, not as blunt—then spent more time than he wanted to admit attempting to spear the fish.

After failing at his fishing opportunity, Mak examined the coiled snare wire hanging from his grubby jeans' belt loop. Perhaps he could fashion a snare of his own and hunt some small pig or deer?

No sooner had he thought of that, than he remembered the injury sustained by the panther. Eating a kill that Mother Wolf had hunted was one thing—but performing the execution himself? Mak didn't think he had the stomach for that. He would have to go hungry for yet another day.

WITHOUT THE RAINS, each night was more comfortable than the last. Mak experimentally howled at night, hoping to hear a reply, but after three nights of silence he decided the wolves had taken their own safe path.

Aside from waking one night screaming as a scorpion explored his chest, Mak was beginning to feel easier on his own—more relaxed than he had felt since arriving in India.

It was this complacency that almost got him killed.

CHAPTER THIRTY-SEVEN

IT WAS SEVERAL DAYS after he had encountered the panther that Mak woke to find fresh tracks circling the deep tree roots he had nestled down in. It was definitely a big cat, and although he couldn't be sure it was the same animal, he recalled Anil talking about how solitary they were, so he assumed it must be the same beast.

Was it following him?

Mak promised himself he would be more vigilant and his eyes strayed to the trees as he walked. In doing so he didn't spot the snare hidden in the leaves until his foot snagged it. It was so well camouflaged that he probably wouldn't have noticed it even if he had looked straight at it.

With a whooshing sound, the pulled snare

dislodged the mechanism attaching it to a tree limb that had been forcibly bent toward the ground. The wood flexed back into shape—pulling the cable and yanking Mak high into the air, suspended by his ankle.

The motion had been so sudden that he didn't even know what had happened. One second he was walking, then the next he was suspended upside down by one leg, gently revolving in a circle.

His ankle throbbed agonizingly as he flailed in the air. The cable had torn through his jeans, and his weight was making the wire dig into his flesh.

Mak screamed, then looked at his leg as he hung upside down.

He could see that he was bleeding, and his leg was numb.

"HELP!"

He called out several more times, hoping that the poachers were still close by, but it was soon apparent that their snares were designed to slowly kill their helpless victims, who would then be collected days or even weeks later. He'd seen documentaries about this: The trappers would hope to catch rare animals for their pelts, not for food. Their deaths were always slow and painful.

Mak had no desire to be counted as their next victim and didn't consider himself helpless. He had something most other animals didn't: fingers.

Crunching his stomach, he managed to bend his body enough for him to catch the dangling cable in one hand. He was impressed—back home he would have counted a sit-up as an achievement. His father had always accused him of being lazy, yet out here the jungle had toughened him up.

He wondered if he would recognize himself in the mirror . . .

Putting such vain thoughts aside, Mak strained against the dangling cable to ease his weight from the snare and used his other hand to slip his foot from the loop. Then, suspended by the cable with both hands, he looked down and dropped.

The pain from his injured foot as it struck the ground felt like an electric shock jolting through his body, and Mak had tears in his eyes as he rolled on the jungle floor in agony. His breathing came in sharp stabbing fits and he had to force himself not to hyperventilate.

Eventually he calmed down and the sharp pain turned into a continuous throb.

He reasoned that it was better to feel something than nothing. He stood, gingerly testing his weight on his injured leg. It hurt, but he could stand enough to limp to a copse of bamboo.

Putting his strength into tearing up a stem, Mak was able to form a crutch. It was enough to take the weight off his leg, but it made progress difficult.

One moment was all it had taken for calamity to ensue. He was angry; the poachers were one element of civilization he had no wish to encounter again.

CHAPTER THIRTY-EIGHT

THE REST OF THE DAY was miserable. The heat prickled Mak's skin, and swarms of gnats formed living clouds he was forced to stumble through, often inhaling lungfuls of the insects.

It was toward the end of the day, as he felt increasingly sorry for himself, that Mak saw something in the trees ahead.

He stopped, puzzled.

It appeared to be a dead creature slumped over a low branch. His first thought was that he was witnessing the handiwork of poachers. He warily drew closer before he realized it was a large spotted deer, a chital, sporting backswept antlers. From the razor-like scratches along its flank it looked like a panther kill.

With every sense alert, Mak limped closer. The last thing he wanted to do was step on the tail of a sleeping panther. Now he was under the carcass and there was still no sign of the hunter. He was so close he could see that half the body had been eaten, and a mass of black flies had begun to congregate on the exposed flesh.

Unable to climb the tree due to his leg, Mak used the bamboo stick to poke the body down. It took several attempts before it slowly slid from the branch, crashing to his feet in a swarm of flies.

Mak knelt at the body and began to pull at the tender morsels inside, the ones the flies had not yet reached and which he knew tasted best. It had felt like a lifetime since he'd last shared meat with the wolves, and the change of diet was welcome. He could almost convince himself that his entire body felt recharged, although the feeling was soon swamped by an intense wave of sleepiness.

And so another day came to an end, and Mak, finding refuge against a fallen log, fell asleep wondering if perhaps the panther had actually left the food as a thank-you for saving its life.

VOICES!

Mak's eyes flicked open; he was instantly alert. Reflexes kicked in and he rolled into a crouch, prepared to react. His leg ached, but it took his weight. That was a bonus—but what had woken him?

There it was again—distant murmuring, as if

people were arguing. Mak cupped his hands behind his ears and slowly turned his head until the sound came into sharper relief.

Mak bolted through the undergrowth, ignoring the pain from his leg in his desperation.

"Hey! Over here!" he yelled as the talking rose in volume.

He stumbled down a hill, gaining momentum as he burst through grass twice as tall as he was—and into an open clearing.

There were no people arguing. Instead, there was an enormous sloth bear, with a thick, shaggy coat. Standing on its hind legs as it stretched—and three times taller than Mak—it was giving a constant gruff growl as it reached for the overhanging branches.

The most dangerous thing anybody can do is startle a hungry bear—and that's exactly what Mak had just done.

CHAPTER THIRTY-NINE

THE HUGE SLOTH BEAR dropped back onto its four legs and extended its jaws so wide Mak could have fit his head inside them. It bellowed, the foul-smelling saliva splattering over Mak's face, forcing him to step backward. He tripped over a branch and fell heavily on his backside.

The bear shook its head, its black shaggy fur fluffing up to make it appear larger. Pushing its white muzzle in the direction of the boy, it sniffed heavily before roaring once more. It raised a paw the size of a plate, tipped with claws bigger than the panther's, and brought it down toward the boy.

Mak rolled aside as the paw shredded the bush he had been leaning against. With nowhere to go, he sprang for the tree, his feet and hands finding supports that allowed him to rapidly climb to the nearest branch.

"You crazy bear! Leave me alone!"

He peered down at the creature, which was now snuffling at the base of the tree. It peered at him, head tilted to the side as its ears twitched. Mak instinctively growled back, making a noise he had never heard before. It sounded angry and loud—Mak was impressed with himself.

The bear reared, massive paws gripping around the trunk. Mak hoped that the bear wouldn't be able to reach him up there and settled back to wait for the animal to lose interest.

Instead, it raised a back paw and experimentally hoisted itself up. To Mak's horror the sloth bear began to ascend, not with a lumbering slow pace, but with the speed of a skilled climber. In moments it had reached Mak's limb, and a paw lashed out—scraping the bark between his legs.

Mak jumped for the branch above, catching it with both hands, and hauled his legs clear just as the bear's jaws snapped beneath him. Hanging upside down on the branch, Mak twisted his body until he was right-side up, then pushed higher into the thicker branches.

Still the sloth bear pursued him, but the thicker branches that Mak's slender frame could weave through proved an effective barrier between him and the bear.

Panting hard, Mak plucked a fruit from the branch nearest his head and threw it at the bear.

"Take that!"

Mak swiped at a fat fly as it buzzed past his face. Then another . . . and another. With the gradual realization straight out of a nightmare, Mak saw that they were not flies—but bees.

He turned to see he had backed up against a hive the size of his own body. Its dimpled surface was a seething mass of bees as they emerged to protect their home.

Bees now crawled all over him. His hands, his face, tickling his ears. He clamped his mouth shut to stop them from crawling in, but felt them around his nose. There were now so many on him, he could feel their collective weight. Still he hadn't been stung, and he had a vague recollection that not all bees had stingers. However, being suffocated by them was not exactly a fun alternative.

The hive shifted position with a drawn-out tearing noise. When Mak had leaned his weight against it, the delicate fist-sized section that attached it to the tree trunk had partially torn away. Now unable to hold its own weight, the hive was slowly detaching . . .

CHAPTER FORTY

MAK FLINCHED as the hive dropped, bouncing from the branch he was sitting on before tumbling away past the bear below. As one, the bees swarming Mak dive-bombed in pursuit, following their home in a pulsing, black living cloud.

The hive cracked in three sections as it struck the ground, issuing a golden trickle of honey across the grass. The bear hooted in delight, sliding effortlessly down the trunk in order to shove its muzzle into the sticky mess. Protected by thick fur, the bear had no issue with the bees that angrily swarmed as it ate their home.

Mak watched, impressed, as the bear made short work of the glistening combs. Defeated, the bees dispersed—following their fleeing queen, until the drone that had filled Mak's ears subsided into nothing more than the soft crunching of the sloth bear devouring the remaining honeycomb. The bear's huge tongue was lapping up every morsel of the golden syrup, and the scent of sweet honey reached Mak's nostrils. His mouth began to water.

Appetite sated, the bear glanced up at Mak and gave two grunts of acknowledgment as it licked its lips before shambling off across the clearing and disappearing into the forest.

"You're most welcome," Mak called after it.

Feeling foolish and suddenly alone, Mak clambered down the tree and examined the broken hive. There were a few traces of honey the greedy bear had missed, so he scooped them with his finger and savored the taste in his mouth. His tongue exploded with delight, and his head swam with the sudden sugar rush.

"That's amazing honey," he declared to several colorful butterflies that had landed on the hive to soak up any sugary residue.

The large clearing gave Mak the opportunity to check his position against the sun. As far as he could tell, he needed to follow the trail of destruction left by the bear. Mak reluctantly followed, making a mental note to keep vigilant for any sign that the animal might decide to turn on him again.

He reckoned that the small scoops of honey were

the best breakfast he'd had in his life and felt a spring in his step as he hopped between the giant ursine paw prints in the ground. He even began to whistle a jaunty tune, which is something he would never have dreamed of doing at home.

CHAPTER FORTY-ONE

THE FOLLOWING DAYS unfolded in much the same way. Mak limped after the sloth bear as closely as he dared. The animal looked old, and Mak nicknamed him Shambler due to the long, unkempt fur that swung like a pendulum from its flanks.

Every so often Shambler would stop and glance over his shoulder at Mak. Satisfied there was no threat from this little moving object, the bear would continue on, tolerating its follower.

Mak was pleasantly surprised to discover the grumpy sloth bear was in fact a very useful teacher. Shambler spent a couple of hours scratching his flanks against a rough tree, while plucking long oval fruit from another tree and devouring them whole. Once the bear moved on, Mak tried the fruit. The green skin was bitter, so he spat that out, but the soft yellow flesh inside was delightful. He didn't recognize the fruit, but the taste was undoubtedly papaya.

A termite nest was next on the menu, Shambler's broad paws scooping into it with ease, making room for his deft tongue, which lapped up dozens of insects at a time. Mak was less inclined to follow this course, but dutifully put his hand on the nest and allowed the small insects to cover his hand.

Steeling himself, Mak sucked several termites from his finger. The sensation of them running around his mouth was awful, so he immediately used his tongue to crush them against the roof of his mouth. He was rewarded with a citrus flavour that had a hint of a rather tasty spice. It was formic acid from the ant, and Mak liked it a lot.

Mak decided it was worthwhile polishing off the remaining termites on his hand with two broad licks of the tongue before following Shambler for dessert.

Dessert came in the form of another beehive, this one wedged into the Y of a tree. The bear had already scrambled up and was crunching through the papery shell, oblivious to the angry bees all around, as Mak arrived at the crime scene.

A fist-size chunk of comb fell to the ground and Mak darted to scoop it up before retreating to a safe distance and scrambling up a boulder to eat. This batch of honey tasted better than the last, and all too soon it had been eaten. While Mak missed the company of the wolves, he had to admit life with Shambler came with an improved menu.

Another day passed. Termites were replaced with grubs clawed from the ground; papaya with a football-size jackfruit. Mak used the snare wire to saw through the tough spiky skin, revealing the orange delight beneath.

With his eyes closed, Mak could smell a welcome combination of pineapple and banana, and the new taste made him smile. Half a jackfruit was more than enough to fill him for most of the day.

THE UNLIKELY DUO HEADED in a southwestern direction each day, and each night they slept apart but close enough for Mak to hear the great bear's bouts of snoring.

Mak was amazed that the bear was continuing to lollop in the same direction that he was wanting to travel himself. He wondered if the jungle was somehow beginning to reward him for his courage.

One day Shambler led him to a river.

Mak was cautious around water ever since the crocodile incident; however, this broad river, with its stony shore, was a watering place for a herd of deer. They eyed Shambler and Mak warily, heads bobbing up from the water in turn, but the newcomers were judged not to be a threat.

The bear splashed through the shallow river,

while Mak stooped to drink. His eyes automatically scanned the prints at the water's edge, and he felt a thrill to see familiar panther tracks. He scanned the trees and could have sworn he felt eyes upon him . . . but concluded it was probably his imagination playing tricks.

CHAPTER FORTY-TWO

IT WAS A LAZY AFTERNOON when Mak began to question exactly *where* the bear was heading. The jungle was changing around them in ways Mak couldn't quite put his finger on. The chatter of parrots in the treetops increased in volume, as did the occasional howls of monkeys who were no more than flitting shadows in the distance.

Emerging in a wide clearing filled with vivid blue flowers, Mak got to see the playful side of the crotchety bear. Shambler ran through the clearing, intentionally startling thousands of butterflies that took to the air in a bloom of color. Both Mak and Shambler watched the kaleidoscopic swirl with delight before the butterflies settled back on the flowers. At no time did the bear attempt to swat or eat them, and Mak felt a deep respect for the wise old animal.

So it was with a heavy heart that Mak stumbled across another poacher's snare. He would have walked right past it, as Shambler had done, if the unnaturally straight line of wire stretching to the tree branches above hadn't caught his attention.

Mak felt a surge of anger at the thought of his gentle companion being caught in the trap, and unleashed his rage as he dismantled the snare and threw the mechanism to the ground.

IT WAS LATER THAT same day that, in a break between the trees to the side, Mak saw kites circling in the sky. Anil had told him that the birds often circled dead prey or easy food from the village. The birds' presence *could* mean a village. He paused—or maybe even a poaching camp. Either would mean a way home.

Mak was surprised to see that Shambler had stopped ahead of him, turned, and was watching him—as if sensing Mak's indecision about whether to follow the bear, or head toward the kites.

Even the slimmest chance to go home had to be pursued. The time had come for him to part ways with his teacher. Shambler hadn't been exactly sociable or affectionate; however, as Mak raised his hand to the bear, he felt sad.

The sloth bear had been a firm companion in his own way.

With a final gruff grunt, Shambler turned away

and disappeared into the jungle. And just like that, Mak was alone once more—yet he still had the same strange feeling of being watched.

Mak took in every shadow and lurking place the jungle had to offer, but saw nothing. The birds were still chattering louder than ever, rather than falling silent as they did when a predator was around. He shook off the feeling and headed toward the kites.

As he drew nearer, the trees seemed to thin out a little, and Mak began to wonder if he had finally reached the edge of the jungle.

Was it possible?

There was certainly something large ahead, near to where the kites were circling.

He quickened his pace, shoving broad leaves aside as they brushed his face. Then the trees thinned out, and Mak couldn't believe what he had stumbled across . . .

CHAPTER FORTY-THREE

THE LIGHT WAS FADING as Mak stared at the city in the jungle.

Turrets stretched above the treetops like stone fingers poised to protect the huge city complex from the jungle beyond.

A huge sweeping wall, held together by ornate columns, stretched four stories high. It would have been the most incredible sight for any weary traveler.

What Mak had first thought to be people standing in alcoves turned out to be statues; ornate gods and deities that were now faded monuments ravaged by the jungle. Whatever vivid colors they had once been adorned with were now covered over by dirt and guano.

Vines smothered the wall and the buildings, searching for gaps between the stone in which they could insert new roots. Trees had grown from under the floor, pushing stones aside in a slow-motion eruption that spanned decades.

The flicker of hope Mak had experienced in the pit of his stomach was instantly extinguished. Nobody was living here.

But that didn't help him shake the sense that he was still being watched . . .

ONE SECTION OF WALL had collapsed in an enormous "V" formation as the ground beneath had slowly eroded, and it now offered Mak the easiest route into the abandoned city. He hopped from one fallen stone block to another until he passed the walls and stepped onto a stone plaza the size of football field.

Here the forest had had a tougher time trying to reclaim the city; instead creepers snaked across the floor, smothering the buildings.

Every footstep Mak took echoed eerily between the dozens of buildings scattered across the plaza. Perhaps they had once been temples or palaces, but time had rendered them empty husks. His foot caught a loose stone, which skittered across the floor, alarming him and making him wince with pain from his old injury.

Mak silently berated himself: Why was he so nervous?

He had survived the perils of the jungle, so what was it about an empty city that was so spooky?

Perhaps it was the way that such a familiar human environment was now deeply bathed in the jungle's shadow: the vines rippling across the floor like dark crevasses, combined with deathly silence, as not a whisper from the jungle beyond penetrated the walls.

The persistent feeling of being spied upon grew with every step, and Mak began to wonder if this was the kind of place the poachers would call their home.

"Is anybody here?" His voice echoed. "I'm lost and need help."

He walked farther across the plaza, holding up the two coils of wire he had taken from the snares.

"I found these out there. Thought they might belong to you. I think animals triggered them, but they must have gotten away." He decided that telling poachers he had been dismantling their traps would not win him any favors.

Still no answer came.

CHAPTER FORTY-FOUR

AHEAD LAY A LARGE SQUARE PIT with steps descending from each side. The base was covered in moss and glistened from the recent rains.

As Mak approached, he saw it had once been a large swimming pool that should have been full after the monsoon rains, but the water had drained away through a huge crack in the floor.

It may not have been filled with water, but it *was* filled with something else.

Snakes.

Hundreds of them.

Mak froze.

Slithering black bodies, some several feet long, criss-crossed one another as they sought out the warm rays of the fading sun. Others crawled up the steps and onto the plaza. Like some hellish optical illusion, Mak suddenly saw that some of what he had taken for vines lacing the plaza were in fact snakes basking in the sun.

He took a wary step back the way he had come— but froze as a snake reared up behind him, hissing as a hood of skin extended behind its head. Mak had seen enough pictures to know what a cobra looked like, and this one looked very angry indeed.

The distant memory of watching a snake charmer on television came to mind, and with few other options, Mak thought it was worth a go. He considered himself an okay singer, although his sister had always insisted he was tone deaf; still, he began yodeling a tune he felt was distinctively Indian and which he hoped would lull the snake.

It didn't.

If anything the snake grew increasingly irritated, and its hood vibrated in an unmistakably threatening manner. Mak immediately shut up.

"No sense of taste," he muttered under his breath.

Despite the peril, Mak didn't feel anxious. The snake had had every opportunity to strike him but hadn't, which indicated that it wasn't looking for a fight. He replayed the last few moments through his head. When he hadn't realized the snakes were there, he had walked carefree through them, and not a single one had attacked. It was only when he'd become tense and tried to step back that things had started to go wrong.

Step back . . .

Of course, he had lumbered closer to the snake and startled it. Even standing, facing it off, could be considered a threat. His eyes darted around and he saw the other snakes were moving sluggishly, more interested in seeking the warmth of the sun than attacking a foe larger than them.

Mak took a long and careful step backward. The cobra hissed more loudly—its head darting forward a couple of inches as if to say, *Yeah, you go!* Mak took another long step back and the cobra lowered to the ground, its interest in him waning.

Mak laughed out loud. "Cool! Okay, I can handle these snakes!"

A sudden hiss close to his ankle told him he had stepped too close to another.

Not wishing to offend the serpents any further, Mak scrambled on his hands and knees up a flight of steep crumbling stone until he was on top of an enormous step that expanded to another elevated—and snake-free—square, surrounded by further-decaying temples and turnip-shaped burial *stupas*.

Huge trees had grown through some of the buildings, and in some cases on top of them. Root structures the size of a truck extended out, forming elaborate veils across building entrances.

At the center of the square was an enormous hole.

Mak warily approached, but this was not another swimming pool. It was circular, and the sides were sheer as it plunged into darkness.

From the depths, Mak could hear the sounds of a mighty torrent, possibly an underground river, which he thought must have made an ideal source of water for the population who once lived here.

Surrounded by plentiful food and water, Mak wondered just what had driven the inhabitants away from such an impressive city. Surely not the snakes?

He shivered, even though sweat clung to his skin and the sun beat down on his brow. Everything around him still possessed an eerie quality, and with it the feeling that he was being watched rose again.

A voice he was beginning to recognize as belonging to his inner primal instinct suggested that he should leave before nightfall. That would mean quickly navigating his way through the cobras in the fading light, then finding somewhere safe to bed down in the jungle beyond. Another voice, this one belonging to his more practical side, pointed out that it was un-likely that the snakes would slither all the way up here at night, and it was doubtful he would find a more secure place than the ruins to spend the night. The place was abandoned, not haunted, he told himself. Besides, he didn't believe in ghosts.

He only hoped that he was right.

CHAPTER FORTY-FIVE

WITH NUMEROUS BUILDINGS to choose from, Mak's selection of sleeping places boiled down to which one had the most open space around it but was still close to a tree. Even though he had almost killed himself falling from a tree, their very presence made Mak feel as if he had guardians watching over him.

He found the ideal building: a small, dome-like structure that had a pair of mighty roots protruding from either side, the tree itself having grown up from within, breaking through the rooftop. Peeking inside the gloomy interior revealed there were few places for something monstrous to hide. Its position on a raised platform appeared to be snake-proof and offered a clear view across the square.

The only downside was the five-story temple

opposite, which had a Swiss-cheese design of archways leading inside, at each of which stood a human-shaped statue. Once, they would have been painted and detailed; now they were pale stone mannequins whose lack of features were somehow more disturbing.

As the sun lowered behind the trees, turning the sky a glorious crimson, there arose a giant *whoosh* of bats, as millions of them took to the skies in silent clouds, mirroring the cobras' slithering formations, except these soared through the sky.

Mak had never seen so many bats before and expected them to be chittering like noisy mice. Instead they were silent except for the leathery rustle of wings. Droves of bats erupted in coordinated bursts that looked like smoke signals being sent to the heavens.

It was almost dark by the time the bats had completed their nightly departure, and Mak was rewarded with the heavens coming alive with stars. With no trees blocking his view, and zero light pollution, the stars appeared to touch the tops of the buildings. Every now and again shooting stars, which in the city he had assumed to be rare things, zipped overhead like tiny fireworks—blazing for several seconds before burning up in the atmosphere.

The sounds of the jungle, which had been muted by the city walls during the daytime, breached them at night, and Mak felt his eyes drooping to the sounds of courting frogs.

• • •

THERE WAS SOMEBODY THERE.

Mak didn't know what had woken him but he was certain somebody had been standing on the edge of the platform looking in his direction. By the time he had sat upright, the figure had vanished, if it had ever been there.

A plump full moon hung high overhead, bathing the city in a cold light.

While in the jungle Mak had glimpsed only slivers of moon, and very little of its light had ever made it through the dense canopy; here it was like a dazzling streetlight. It cast shadows on the stone figures across from him, tricking him into thinking they were moving from the corner of his eye. However, every time he stopped and stared he saw nothing but a stationary statue.

"Get a grip of yourself." His voice echoed from the buildings and was comforting to hear. It was even more comforting *not* getting a response.

Mak settled down again, pushing himself against the giant root that curved perfectly along his body. No sooner had he begun to relax than he heard a noise: a stone dropping, bouncing from the steps before skittering into the square. In the dead of night the sound was amplified unnaturally loud.

Mak's heart was in his throat. There was no breeze so what could have caused it? The list of possibilities raced through his mind—rats, foraging squirrels, birds, bats—all seemed reasonable options.

Or ghosts?

Mak bolted upright again—and this time he was certain what he saw was no trick of the light. Somebody was crouching on the corner step of the temple opposite. It was too far away to make out any detail, but they hadn't been there moments before.

In the moonlight, Mak could see the figure's head turn and stare in his direction.

But more chillingly was the way the moonlight fell onto its pure white body.

CHAPTER FORTY-SIX

JUMPING TO HIS FEET took Mak only a second—but in that time the shape had vanished. He clenched his fists, unsure just how he was supposed to fight a spirit.

His second instinct was to hide in the shadows offered by the nearby tree. He crouched down, making himself a less obvious target, and with the solid mass behind him, felt safe that no phantom could stalk up from behind.

Mak's stomach knotted with fear as he peered over his cover. A pale blur was rapidly ascending the temple, moving in long zigzag motions from ledge to ledge. Then the white figure was atop the temple and bathed in full-moon light. Mak could now make out the shape of a hunched figure, resting its weight on both long arms that were ramrod straight in front of it. Mak stared as intently as he could in the low light, adjusting his position to get a better look.

The phantom's body was covered in fur. Pure white fur. Mak didn't move as the creature gave a series of short throaty barks.

Mak breathed a sigh of relief under his breath. "You stupid monkey." The specter was a macaque monkey, a particularly large specimen, cloaked in shaggy white fur. Mak judged it to be as big as he was.

He was pretty certain that it wasn't a ghost-monkey either.

There was little point in hiding if the monkey knew where he was, so Mak began to stand—but stopped mid-crouch when he saw movement in the shadowy alcoves. More macaques appeared, of more regular sizes, and their numbers swelled out of the temple in stealthy silence.

Most kept to the balconies below, the more alpha specimens joining their Pale King on the roof—but all of them were looking toward Mak.

In the moonlight, Mak could see heads bob and sway as the monkeys peered at him. Then a combined series of low grunts and whines rose from the assembled throng. It was not an endearing noise, and Mak felt the harsh cough-like sounds were challenges.

He slowly realized he had stumbled into their territory. An intruder.

The entire situation felt like an army massing its

ranks, but Mak couldn't work out why the monkeys were not simply attacking. That's when he noticed the primates on the lower temple steps were bent forward, noses peering off the edge and bottoms wagging in the air as they inspected the square—most of which was covered by the temple's shadow.

One macaque flinched as a shadow—cast by a fellow troop member farther up the temple—moved. The lower monkey gave a warning howl.

Snakes. They were afraid of the snakes, and even in a braying army the lead soldiers would have second thoughts about charging across a plaza of deadly cobras. This gave Mak a head start. He knew that he had to leave the ruined city—and fast.

Scurrying on his hands and knees, almost as quickly as the monkeys, Mak kept low and vaulted over the wide tree root, away from the temple. Behind the *stupa*, the area was black with shadow, but Mak couldn't risk slowing down for fear of snakes.

He felt pools of cool mud splash across his feet and hoped the cobras would prefer a drier place to sleep as the nightly temperatures dropped.

Ahead was an oblong-shaped building with one crumbling side that provided makeshift steps to the roof. Mak hopped from each fallen stone to the next, using his hands to haul himself up the larger ones.

He was panting for breath by the time he reached the summit and looked around.

The city walls seemed distant and from this vantage point still intact all the way around, save for the gap through which he'd entered. The only problem was that the exit lay *beyond* the monkey temple, meaning he would have to circumnavigate them.

He had been listening for signs of pursuit and prayed the silence meant the monkeys had forgotten about him. His hope was shattered when there arose behind him such a clamor of whoops and screams echoing across the stone city that his blood turned cold.

He could just see the top floors of the temple and the rush of movement as dozens of macaques poured down. In the moonlight it gave the illusion that the temple was melting.

Their Pale King sat on his haunches looking directly at Mak and hooting feverishly. Mak realized his error—by standing on the rooftop he had become a clear target, and now the mob was in pursuit.

CHAPTER FORTY-SEVEN

TAKING THE FALLEN STONES two at a time, Mak bounded down the opposite side of the building. Landing on the smooth plaza floor, he sprinted toward the darkness afforded by another clutch of smaller buildings.

He glanced over his shoulder in time to see the wave of gibbering macaques surge over the ruins like ants, their previous trepidation about the snakes now replaced by a bloodthirsty desire to hunt the intruder. Mak had no illusions that being caught would mean an instant death sentence, torn apart by the brutes.

He could see that they were massing toward the oblong building as he arced around the plaza, and was grateful that he was managing to put some distance between them, while slowly doubling back toward the break in the wall. His plan might just work . . .

A repeated screeching noise made him glance over his shoulder again. A macaque had spotted Mak and it was now hopping madly, screaming at its companions. It took only a moment before the hundred-strong army took heed and began to cartwheel toward him.

Mak lost sight of them as he slipped through a narrow gap between some buildings that had been constructed behind the larger temples, perhaps once offering accommodation for those who worked there.

Here the ground was slick and muddy; sheltered from the direct rays of the sun, it had not yet had time to dry out, if indeed it ever would. Mak guessed that there was no way he could outrun his pursuers, especially not in a straight line once he emerged in the plaza. He would have to out-think them.

His first impulse was to hide, but he had been in the jungle long enough now to know that any animal's keen sense of smell would instantly detect him. He needed to blend in . . .

No sooner had the thought struck him than Mak threw himself into the thick oozing mud. He rolled this way and that to ensure he was covered. He was thankful he couldn't see in the darkness, but there was a distinct smell of poop among the mud. The mud slid over his ears, mouth, and nose—the stench was repulsive.

Satisfied he was completely covered, Mak stood— his bare feet slipping in the filth—and darted inside a gap in the nearest wall—just as the macaques surged over the buildings behind him.

Mak pressed himself against a stone column and held his breath—in part so they couldn't hear his panting, but mostly because he didn't want to inhale the smell of the mud.

Outside, the monkeys thundered past, but their pace slowed. No longer able to hear or see their quarry, they suspected he had hidden.

The sound of curious grunts filled the air as the primates stopped and began searching the area outside the building. One sat on its haunches beside the gap Mak had slipped through, and began scratching itself.

Mak now saw the flaw in his plan. The macaques were spreading out beyond the buildings, making it impossible for him to slip through their ranks.

His only exit was now blocked.

He allowed his eyes to adjust to the darkness around him. Some moonlight lanced in through cracks, revealing a surprisingly large chamber. Scores of columns supported the high ceiling. These had been protected from the ravages of the weather, and Mak could just make out carvings of monkeys and serpents adorning them.

He was inside one of the temples.

Having gained access through a crack in the wall, he reasoned that there should be a proper exit elsewhere. If he could find it.

Mak crept forward—his foot skittering a pebble across the chamber. It echoed loudly, and the macaque guarding his entrance peered inside.

With his toes throbbing, Mak pressed himself back against a column. After a moment, he risked peeking behind him.

The macaque had entered the temple. Mak could just see the creature's silhouette, head tilted upward as it sniffed the air.

It slowly advanced, now hunched forward on its front arms as its nose weaved across the floor, searching for the scent of man. Mak's decision to bathe in mud just might have saved his life.

The ape was now on the opposite side of his pillar. Mak pressed himself flat and slowly edged in the opposite direction. His foot caught a rock, something the size of a football that caused him to stumble.

It was a fatal mistake.

CHAPTER FORTY-EIGHT

WITH A HISS the macaque vaulted around the column, and even in the dim light Mak could see its lips were pulled back, baring huge and lethal incisors.

Mak was still stumbling on the rock, and now, forced backward, he tripped hard and landed on his backside. At the same moment he felt a rush of air as the monkey's paw lashed past where his head had been. The terrible sound of claws raking stone told Mak that his face would have been torn in two.

With a screech, the macaque pivoted around so that it could bite him. Mak felt slobber splash across his face. His hands reached instinctively for some sort of a weapon—anything to ward the beast off.

He touched the wire cables he'd taken from the poachers' traps hanging from his side. Without thinking, he pulled one free, flicking it like a whip. The steel cable lashed around the macaque's leg.

The furious monkey howled in pain as it was whipped, but Mak didn't care. He caught the end of the traveling cable. It stung his palm, but he didn't let go—instead he heaved all his weight backward just as the macaque was preparing to leap at him, and he pulled.

The cable tightened, forcing the startled monkey to stumble as its leg refused to move in the direction it wanted to go. The beast howled in confusion as Mak circled it, yanking the wire ever tighter.

Mak wrapped the end he had been holding around a root that was growing through the wall and hurried off in the opposite direction, leaving the monkey howling. It was just a matter of time before another ape came to investigate the disturbance, or the macaque wriggled free.

Although Mak couldn't see, the temple around him seemed to yawn wide into the darkness. He ran around one fat, onion-shaped pillar and then suddenly stopped in his tracks.

Before him was a giant monkey, some six feet tall. Its snarling face was lit by moonlight seeping through a hole in the roof. It was only on second glance that Mak realized this was an enormous statue of a monkey god, its four huge arms extended in prayer, a massive tail slinking around the columns and up to the dark ceiling above.

Mak didn't need time to think. Every church and temple he had ever gone into always had the central icon facing the doorway. He spun around and, sure enough, saw a glimmer of light from the main entrance. He ran toward it, stopping as he drew near. He pressed his body against the wall and peered out at what lay beyond.

It was the wide plaza with the cobra-filled swimming pool in the middle. The distant fallen wall was just visible in the gloom and, beyond, the welcoming dark of the jungle beckoned.

Just one long sprint to freedom and he was certain he'd be able to lose his attackers in the jungle. He braced himself, taking several long breaths. He edged out of the doorway to the top of the moss-covered steps leading into the plaza. He could see dark shapes languishing across the stone floor—but whether they were sleeping cobras or merely harmless roots he couldn't tell.

He counted down in his mind—*Three, two . . .*

And just then he became aware of heavy breathing over his shoulder. He cocked his head back, just enough to make out the enormous white macaque hunched over the temple entrance. Even from the corner of his eye, Mak could make out its malevolent expression, the scar that ran across one eye to its nose—a sign of a previous battle for dominance— and the string of saliva that now dribbled down across Mak's back.

One single pounce and Mak would fall in a torrent of claws and fangs. There was nowhere left to run. Surprisingly, Mak didn't feel afraid. He had faced many dangers in the wild now and had survived them all, although to be outwitted by a monkey would add insult to injury. If only he could distract the animal . . .

Then an idea came to him.

Mak slowly turned, attempting to make every gesture seem unthreatening. A vague recollection that one shouldn't make eye contact with primates came to mind.

Mak's eyes darted away, not wishing to either provoke the beast or see the attack that would kill him. Instead, his gaze fell to his hand as he slowly drew something from his pocket.

The Pale King's head turned, and its threatening grunts faded as it saw the coin dancing through Mak's fingers.

The moonlight caught the shiny surface of the coin in tiny bursts as it cascaded down Mak's knuckles, then up again in an almost hypnotic manner. It held the monkey's attention for now, but with each pass the coin was losing its sheen due to the mud on Mak's fingers.

He caught movement beyond the white beast—the remainder of the troop were silently gathering along the steep temple walls, all looking down in fascination at the flickering light in Mak's hand. More appeared along the side of the temple, inadvertently cutting off Mak's direct path to the gap in the wall. He would have to flee in the opposite direction.

Running out of time, Mak tensed—then tossed the coin high in the air to one side. As one, the monkeys' heads turned to track it—and Mak jumped down the temple steps.

He had just a few seconds' lead on them—but landed on both feet as the Pale King howled in fury. Mak sprinted across the plaza—his naked feet kicking as he tried to dodge and jump both the vines and the lethal web of snakes.

He was moving quickly—too fast for the serpents as they hissed and reared in his wake. With no cloud coverage, the night was chillier than usual, which meant the snakes' reactions were sluggish. Mak focused on his destination ahead, the large raised square.

Throwing caution to the wind, the macaques charged after him—but in the wake of the startled snakes, they suffered terrible injuries. The angry growls quickly turned to yelps of pain as the cobras struck. Many of the leading monkeys suffered multiple bites and staggered woozily before crumpling to the ground, howling wildly. The other monkeys wisely hesitated as they looked on from the temple.

The Pale King roared in fury. The monkeys scattered left and right, keeping to the raised areas as they circled around the snake-filled plaza, closing in on their prey in a wide pincer movement.

Mak had postponed his death by perhaps a minute. His flight had taken him farther away from the gap in the wall, and he felt he was now running in circles as the ranks of his enemy cut off his only line of escape.

Then a familiar howl echoed across the city, a long, piercing cry that shocked Mak to his core and froze him in his tracks.

And then in an instant it lifted Mak's spirits like nothing ever before. The advancing mob hesitated in confusion, heads snapping in every direction to spot this new threat.

Mak's heart soared as the familiar shape of Mother Wolf appeared on top of a pyramidal structure, her head tilted back as she howled again—perfectly silhouetted against the full moon.

CHAPTER FORTY-NINE

IN RESPONSE, Mak howled back and began shaking with joy when Mother Wolf, accompanied by Yip and Itch, scrambled down and joined his side. Their timing couldn't have been better. As Mak tore his gaze away from his rescuers, he saw the mighty white macaque was still charging him. While the other monkeys were stricken with fear, their leader sought only blood.

With its jaw extended and huge fangs poised to tear Mak's throat out, the Pale King made a final leap. There was a blur of movement as Mother Wolf accelerated and, with a chilling snarl, bounded into the macaque's side. They both tumbled to the floor, rolling over and over toward the lip of the raised square, as teeth gnashed and claws gouged.

A flower of blood stained the Pale King's side as

the wolf bit down—but Mother Wolf yelped as the monkey pounded its fists into her head. Yip and Itch growled as menacingly as they could manage, keeping the remaining monkeys at bay.

More painful yelps came from Mother Wolf as she was lifted into the air by the Pale King, the macaque's hands around her throat, feet firmly planted in her chest. Rage surged through Mak, and just as the wolf was hurled against the stone floor, he charged.

The Pale King stood on its hind legs, raising its arms to strike down on the prone wolf. With his back to Mak, he didn't see the boy closing in. The monkey only half-turned when he heard the human's battle cry—but by then it was too late.

Mak shouldered into the monkey, thrusting his elbow in hard until he heard something crack. The macaque bellowed in pain and tried to turn around, its feet tripping over the wolf. The Pale King tumbled off the edge of the plaza, landing awkwardly with a cry of pain.

In the moonlight, Mak could just see one of the macaque's arms hung limp as he tried to roll to his feet. He could also see the floor was moving beneath the monkey.

Snakes.

The high-pitched screeches of pain forced Mak to look away as a mass of cobras swamped the Pale King. The searing pain from the snakebites didn't last long as the enormous quantity of poison surged through the white macaque, seizing its heart. Mak looked back to see only the Pale King's hand poking through the seething black mass.

He knelt at Mother Wolf's side and ran his hand across her body. She was bleeding. Mak hoped it was only from scratches rather than anything fatal.

The wolf licked his face, causing him to smile despite the jeopardy they were still in.

Then the wolf rolled to her feet, immediately rounding on the monkey troop who had stepped forward to watch their leader die.

She gave a deep growl, slowly backing toward her pups. Mak stayed by her side and looked around for an opportunity to escape. It was worse than before. While one wave of monkeys had stopped to watch the battle, the others had circled them, completing their pincer movement.

There was no getting away from the hard facts: Mak and the wolves were trapped.

Gibbering confusion ran through the macaques as they looked at their fallen leader—then a large gray male strode forward, this one sporting a disgusting growth on the side of his cheek. He roared at Mak.

Concerned now for the wolves' safety rather than his own, Mak scooped up Itch and Yip and backed toward an enormous hole in the ground. Maybe this dip in the ground could hide their retreat.

Then Mak noticed something unusual about the hole. He could hear the roar of a river below, and the noise was coming straight up from the chasm below him. It was an enormous well.

He whistled to Mother Wolf, who followed his gaze to the well, then to the mass of slavering macaques around them.

Mak took a deep breath, held the two pups tight, then jumped into the well, hoping that he hadn't sealed their fate.

CHAPTER FIFTY

A FEW SECONDS of falling, then a splash.

The frigid water felt like needles of ice thrust into Mak's nerves. A stream of bubbles involuntarily blew from his mouth as his whole body convulsed. He desperately tried to hold on to the two pups, but their wriggling forms slipped from his grasp, allowing him to use his hands to stabilize himself.

It was absolutely pitch-black in the well, and Mak couldn't even tell which way was up—but then he felt the powerful tug of the underground river he'd leaped into. He'd been thrust into water so much during his jungle journey that by now he had learned the vital lesson—don't panic. By simply not moving and allowing the current to carry him, he was saving precious oxygen.

Now as relaxed as he could be, Mak's other senses attempted to compensate. His body was alive with adrenaline, and he could just feel the tickle of air bubbles creeping over his body, all moving in the same direction. Reorienting himself, he felt the same bubbles travel up his spine and neck.

Up . . .

Mak kicked his legs to chase the bubbles, and his head popped out of the water.

He had just enough time to gulp a fresh new breath before the raging surface splashed him in the face and the underground river's current dragged him down again. In that brief respite he had also heard the welcome sound of furious whining—at least the wolves were with him.

After several more cycles of gulping air and being yanked back down, Mak noticed a pale source of light ahead. He kicked powerfully to the surface using both his arms and legs. His head shot out of the water at the very same moment his body struck a rock beneath the surface and he was surprised to find himself suddenly catapulted out of the water and flailing through the air.

Mak was confused and lost all sense of direction as he fell for what felt like forever—eventually impacting on more water below with even more force. He disappeared under the surface once more, until his natural buoyancy carried him back to the surface. He swam as hard as he could, ignoring the throbbing pain in his backside from where he had hit the rock. Breaking the surface once more, he gulped in a deep breath and took in his new surroundings.

The underground river had emerged from a circular hole halfway up a cliff face. The torrent had spat him out into the air, and he had tumbled down, landing in a large plunge pool that then snaked away as a river through the jungle.

Mak swam to the shore and was relieved to feel soft sand beneath his hands and knees as he crawled out. The moon was bright and the grass in the clearing around the pool rippled with silver flecks. He scanned the river, searching with all his might for any sign of the wolves.

But there was nothing.

He called out in a loud whisper: "Yip? Itch? Can you hear me?"

Nothing.

Then suddenly he saw the three wolves emerge from the water. His heart leaped!

And they looked in better shape than he did. Mother Wolf was nuzzling her two pups, sniffing for any sign of injury and ushering them out of the water. Then all three shook themselves dry before Mother Wolf crossed to Mak and licked his face too.

He laughed, throwing his arms around the animal in a tight hug.

"Thank you for coming after me," he said with heartfelt relief. "Thank you!"

Mother Wolf's snout gently pushed his arm away and she shook her fur again on the banks, splashing Mak with water that stank of dog. He didn't mind; he was too busy scruffing the heads of Itch and Yip as they stood on his chest, both trying to lick his face. He didn't want this moment to end.

MAK SLOWLY AWOKE to warm rays of sunlight caressing his face. Birds twittered from all around him, while the constant dull roar of the waterfall provided a soothing soundtrack. The two pups were on either side of him, their warm furry bodies feeling like hotwater bottles. He was content not to move.

He didn't recall falling asleep, and hadn't moved far from the water's edge. His backside and leg throbbed from where he had struck the rock and then fallen into the plunge pool. With the minimum of movement he could see a nasty purple bruise on the side of his leg.

Blue-feathered parrots flittered from the trees, paying no attention to the unlikely wolf/human family below.

Mak scratched his head, noticing for the first time that his hair was longer than usual. Definitely longer than it was before and after winter break, having avoided the hairdresser. That hinted that he had been a month or more in the wild.

No longer were his thoughts darkly pondering whether his parents were alive. Instead he was now wondering if they thought *he* was still alive. Had they given up on him? Had they held his funeral? He wondered just how many of his classmates would have turned up to that. Probably not many, but the thought put a wry, morbid smile on his face.

But then Mak experienced a wave of sorrow for his mother and father. They must have gone through hell thinking he had died in the jungle, no doubt blaming themselves for dragging him out here against his wishes.

He slowly sat up, trying not to disturb the pups, who stretched and yawned beside him as they woke. Mak took everything in. How could he *not* want to be here? It was as if somebody had sculpted paradise and dropped him in it. Sure, killer crocs, rabid monkeys, and unforgiving poachers' traps were not very welcome, but every incident had made him feel *alive*. And the importance of family had been drilled into him at every turn, whatever form it took.

Looking up, he saw Mother Wolf returning with a fresh kill, a young forest pig, and Mak's stomach rumbled at the thought of a filling meal.

CHAPTER FIFTY-ONE

FOR SEVERAL DAYS AFTERWARD, life appeared to fall back into the familiar comfortable routine. Waking to a fresh meal, then wandering to pastures new—except Mak couldn't shake the feeling that there was now a sense of purpose to Mother Wolf's actions.

She would slink off into the forest, as if scouting ahead. Sometimes she would disappear for several hours—although Mak had long since lost any accurate measure of time—before returning and ushering Mak and the pups to follow her.

At first Mak put it down to the wolf's anxiety in case the monkeys had decided to pursue them, but the farther they moved from the temple the more her odd behavior increased.

It was as light was fading at the end of another quiet day that Mak saw something that quickened his pulse. They had reached a shallow river, and the pups had sprawled themselves out on a large rock to bathe in the sun. Mak knelt at the water's edge to drink when he noticed dozens of overlapping tracks in the mud. They were the marks of big, heavy beasts. The cloven prints made him think of cows. While he was wondering if it was possible to have wild cows, he noticed another set of tracks.

Human footprints.

They were unmistakable.

Big, heavy boots with angular soles that had left clean marks in the ground. As best he could tell, there were two people accompanying the herd, but the crisscrossing marks were too confusing for him to be certain. It was clear the people had been walking to the side of the animals, perhaps guiding them. He lost sight of the prints as they disappeared down a narrow hunting track that weaved deeper into the jungle.

It was too late to go careering blind and alone down any hunting paths, so Mak lay with the wolves in the safety offered by a shallow cave in the riverbank and fell into a fitful sleep.

But it was the first time yet that his dreams had been good.

THE NEXT MORNING, Mak didn't feel hungry when breakfast was served. This morning it was a gray langur monkey, and the sight of the wolves tearing into a small human-shaped body was too much for Mak. It was as if a switch had been thrown in his head, and he was suddenly tired of foraging, of eating raw meat, and sleeping in caves. The wilderness had been the ultimate adventure, but now his heart wanted to return home.

For most of the day, Mak led the way down the hunting track as it curved through gentle valleys and around sharp, rocky towers. As the sun reached its highest midday point, they stopped to rest, and Mak discovered not only more traces of the cattle prints, but also those of a panther.

He traced his finger around the fresh paw prints. They were the same size as his old friend's, but Mak didn't waste time looking around. Judging by their condition, they could have been left hours ago.

Toward the end of the day the wolves grew anxious. A hazy mist lent a lazy quality to the light, and Mak could smell the unmistakable scent of woodsmoke. His pulse quickened—he could sense that people were close by.

He took several more steps before stopping. The wolves were no longer following him. They had traveled as far as they dared, deliberately leading him to his own people. Mak walked back to his wolf friends and dropped to his knees. He scratched Yip between the ears, the little pup giving a gurgle of satisfaction. Then he rubbed Itch's tummy until the pup batted him away with its rear paws, indicating there was too much of a good thing.

"You look after each other," he told them. "No more jumping into wells and chasing angry macaques."

Then he turned to Mother Wolf, who was sitting on her back paws, head held regally high as she studied Mak. He slowly extended his hand and ran it along her soft, gray flanks.

"And you. I owe you everything."

His voice cracked and he felt warm tears in his eyes. Something deep inside told him this was likely to be the last time he would see her again. He wished the wolf could talk, and that he could tell her how much he had come to love her.

Mother Wolf's coarse tongue ran across his face, licking away his tears. Then she turned and disappeared down the trail.

Her pups diligently followed. Mak watched, waiting for them to turn around one last time. They didn't.

With a hurting heart, Mak resumed his course

down the pathway. The scent of woodsmoke grew stronger, and as the sunlight dwindled, Mak saw lights through the trees ahead.

It really was time.

He had reached civilization.

CHAPTER FIFTY-TWO

FOUR HUTS made from wood and corrugated-iron roofs were the first signs of civilization Mak had seen in a long while. There was nobody around, but a flickering light came from one of the huts.

Farther off he could see a wood-and-wire enclosure that housed about thirty buffalo. *Not cows*, Mak corrected himself. The docile creatures sported powerful-looking curved horns, but they seemed content eating a stack of greenery that had been piled into their pen.

A small cooking fire sat a little away from the huts, and it was from this that gray smoke drifted from under a cast-iron cooking pot. Excited, Mak started forward, but stopped when he saw what lay through the open door of one of the darker huts.

Rows of animal furs hung drying in the darkness.

Mak could see shades from light brown to black, but was unable to identify the animals they had once belonged to.

His stomach turned when he saw the beautiful black hide of a panther, and he fervently hoped it didn't belong to the graceful animal he had saved. He had longed to find fellow humans, but to be welcomed by poachers was not something he had ever anticipated.

Sudden shouting in Hindi made him start. He turned to see a heavy-set Indian man stepping out of the illuminated hut. Mak's eyes immediately strayed to the rifle the man held under his arm, poised to scare off any intruders, but the barrel dipped when the man caught sight of Mak's face. The man's eyes went wide.

Mak's mouth was dry. "H-hello." He licked his lips and spoke louder. "Do you speak English?"

A tall, thin white man followed his companion from the hut and his eyes grew as big as saucers when he saw Mak. The men exchanged glances before the white man spoke with an Indian accent.

"I speak English, boy." His eyes suspiciously scanned the forest behind Mak. "Why are you out here?"

"I got lost," said Mak, still trying to find his voice. "A boating accident. I was thrown into the river. I lost my parents and . . . I don't know if they are alive. I need to contact them. To go home." Everything was coming out in a rush now.

The two men exchanged another look. The one who spoke gazed into the jungle again. "You are alone? All the way out here?"

Mak nodded. "I've been scavenging food. Walking every day, trying to get out." The white man translated for his companion, whose mouth hung in an "O" of astonishment. "Please, can you help me? I just want to go home."

Eventually the man nodded and beckoned Mak into the hut. "Come inside and eat." As Mak walked past he saw both men's noses wrinkle in disgust. "And get yourself cleaned up," he added.

IN THE WARM YELLOW LIGHT of a kerosene lantern, Mak had stared into the mirror for what seemed like an eternity. The face looking back at him was completely unfamiliar. It was encrusted with grime. His cheeks looked lean, but he could see perfect muscle definition on his arms and chest, and couldn't resist a few superhero poses to flex his muscles.

The white man introduced himself as Gideon, and his companion as Sunil. He insisted that Mak bathe himself behind the huts, using water from a nearby stream warmed over the fire. It took several buckets to remove even a single layer of dirt, but Mak felt better for it.

With no change of clothes, Mak looked forlornly at his own before putting them back on. His once-blue jeans were ripped to the knees and completely frayed. Taking a knife hanging from a hook in the nearest furshed, he cut off the frayed ends to make a pair of shorts. As for his underwear . . . well, that went straight onto the fire in a gust of foul-smelling sparks. His T-shirt was so black and sweat-stained that no trace of the original color remained.

Back inside the hut, Sunil ladled a bowl of steaming hot broth into a bowl. Mak burned his mouth as he guzzled it down. He'd forgotten the delight of cooked food and couldn't hold back a deep belch as he offered his bowl for seconds.

The men studied him with interest, waiting until he had finished his second helping of broth before offering a cup of warm tea to wash it down. Then they asked him to tell his story.

CHAPTER FIFTY-THREE

MAK TALKED for what seemed like hours, recounting his adventures, although he carefully left out any reference to dismantling the poachers' traps or the encounter with the panther. Even when it came to discussing the wolves, he was careful to edit any mention of the pups, fearing for their safety.

As he settled into the story he looked around, staring for long moments as if trying to recall details. What he was in fact doing was taking in the room around him. It wasn't that he didn't trust the men; they seemed friendly enough—but they were undoubtedly hunting endangered animals, and Mak was only too aware that they had not yet contacted anybody to say they had found a missing child. He had spied a radio in the corner, partially covered by a waterproof canvas sheet, but no one had put in a call to announce Mak's reappearance.

That made him wary.

Against another wall was a wooden chest containing several rifles and boxes of ammunition. Sunil closed the lid after Mak's gaze lingered on it a moment too long. Mak tried not to react and continued his tale—the highlights of which Gideon translated into Hindi for Sunil's benefit. Mak paused, then looked Gideon straight in the eye . . .

"Can you use the radio to contact the authorities and tell them I am alive?"

He saw Gideon's eyes flick to the radio. Mak had a feeling the man was going to deny that they possessed a radio, but now he knew Mak had seen it. After a moment's thought, Gideon shrugged.

"Of course. As soon as it is light." He smiled when Mak frowned. "It's solar-powered, so . . ." He gestured to the mosquito net that served as a window. Outside it was inky black.

Mak nodded, but he didn't quite believe the man. He pressed for further information. "How far are we from the nearest town?"

Gideon gave another shrug. "Oh, quite far. It took us several days to get here."

"So what are you doing so far out here?"

Gideon fixed him with a piercing look, his words coming in clipped tones. "We are cattle drivers. Moving those buffalo through from village to village." He didn't blink, as if daring Mak to challenge him.

Mak wondered if they had yet discovered the snares he had dismantled. If so, it wouldn't take a genius to work out he had been the one sabotaging them. For an awkward beat Mak thought Gideon could read the guilt on his face, yet the man didn't level any accusations. Mak forced a smile. "Must be dangerous work out here."

"Oh, it is. One must always be prepared. The wild cannot be trusted. And accidents happen all the time."

It was a blatant threat, but Mak nodded in agreement. "Which is why I can't wait to get back home and leave both of you kind men to continue your important work."

Gideon's lip curled in a partial sneer, but whatever he was about to say never made it to his lips. A low beep suddenly sounded from beneath the canvas radio cover. Sunil swept it aside, revealing not just the radio—which Mak couldn't help but notice had its green power light on—but another, smaller, older device with an oscillating green screen, which was making all the noise.

Sunil spoke rapidly, darting to the weapons chest and pulling out a rifle, no longer concerned if Mak saw what was inside. He spoke rapidly in Hindi, and Gideon jumped to his feet, snatching his rifle from where he had propped it behind the door.

"What's happening?" said Mak in confusion.

"An intruder has broken the tripwire."

Mak's mind raced. An intruder? Could it be another poacher or perhaps the law clamping down on this illegal poaching ring?

"Who?"

"Big cat after the buffalo." Gideon and Sunil ran through the door. "Stay here!"

Mak got as far as standing when Gideon slammed the door closed. He heard metal bolts being drawn on the outside and he dashed for the door.

It wouldn't open—he had been locked inside.

Mak crossed to the window to peer out. He could just make out the forms of the two men hurrying toward the buffalo enclosure, and heard the restless grunts from the beasts as something in the night disturbed them.

Why had they locked him inside? Certainly not for his own safety. Then his eyes fell on the radio and the tantalizing green power light. They had locked him in the same room as the radio.

Mak rushed around the table and examined the radio. It was old and sturdy with a gray LCD screen for selecting the station. A microphone was clipped to the side, attached to the set by a coiling plastic cable that had long ago lost its elasticity.

With a trembling hand he flicked the power switch and the screen came alive with a basic digital display, and with it the speaker made a single electronic *thud* as it powered up.

Mak's hand went for the microphone, his fingers touching the green plastic just as he heard the buffalo bellow outside. Then he heard Sunil shouting in Hindi, followed by the clear crack of a rifle report. The gunfire was immediately answered by a terrifying yowling.

It was a panther.

CHAPTER FIFTY-FOUR

A SECOND GUNSHOT rang out, followed by more shouting and the increasingly anxious murmur of the penned buffalo. Mak hurried to the window and tore the mosquito net aside. He clambered onto the table, almost kicking over the kerosene lamp as he did so. He caught it by the handle just in time, then crawled through the window, dropping to a crouch in the darkness outside.

After the light from inside the cabin, Mak's night vision was shot. He closed his eyes, but could still see the pale afterglow spots of the lamp. He waited impatiently for his eyes to adjust, as the soundscape around him changed. Gideon and Sunil lapsed into silence, and he couldn't hear the panther, although from the noise of the increasingly anxious buffalo he guessed the big cat was not only alive, but still some-where close by.

Mak did not believe for a moment that the men were protecting the buffalo; it was more likely the poor animals had been corralled out here to be used as bait to lure big cats in.

He opened his eyes. His night vision had grown more acute during his time in the jungle, and he was aided by the full moon that was partially obscured by a lone cloud.

Mak could see the poachers on the other side of the pen, hunched low as they peered over the cattle, guns jammed against their shoulders, waiting to shoot a likely target.

Crawling forward, Mak gained a better view around the buffalo pen. He searched the darkness for any sign of the panther. Nothing moved.

Then he saw something that filled him with a burst of hope, quickly followed by dread. A single flashing green LED in the darkness. The last time he had seen that sight was on the collar of a panther. *His* panther. Either the men couldn't see it from where they were, or the light was too dim for them to notice.

Behind the panther was a raised incline of rocks, with more trees on top. Due to the position of the enclosure, it meant the panther was trapped—either he could go through the buffalo, or scramble up the embankment, both of which would make him an easy target.

Mak had to do something. He considered for a moment a return to the weapons chest, but thought it more likely he'd shoot his own foot off than save anybody. Attacking these men would be foolish, but his magic practice had taught him something much more powerful—the art of distraction. A shiny coin wouldn't work with poachers, so it would have to be something much more elaborate.

Moving rapidly on his hands and knees, Mak made his way to the wooden gate that hemmed the buffalo in. It was fastened with a simple loop of rope over a peg. He removed the loop and opened the gate a few inches. One buffalo was looking straight at him, but it didn't take the cue to leave. Clearly, opening the gate would not have the dramatic effect he needed.

The campfire was still burning, the low flame almost nothing more than a glowing charred stick. The empty iron pot still hung on a forked wooden branch above it.

Mak made his way to it, unhooked the pot and checked it was dry inside. Then he took a fistful of dried grass and kindling that had been stacked next to the fire and dropped it inside. He angled the pot to scoop up the embers and gently blew into the pot to stoke the flame. The kindling caught.

Keeping to the shadows, Mak scuttled closer to

the enclosure. The pot was heavy, so gripping the thin handle firmly, he circled his arm, revolving the pot in a sweeping revolution—once, twice . . .

On the third swing he had built up enough momentum to release it. With satisfaction he watched the pot soar over the pen, rebound from a tree and fall into the stack of greenery the poachers had been using to feed the cattle.

Neither man had seen the pot sail overhead, but they heard the crash as it landed. Mak saw both guns swivel in the direction of the noise. At the same moment the dry grass caught fire as the blazing embers spilt over them.

Sunil impulsively pulled the trigger, shooting into the trees.

CHAPTER FIFTY-FIVE

THE COMBINATION of the sudden flames and the rifle's loud report startled the buffalo and, with a bugling cry, they surged forward. The gate swung open before catching on a rock, but that didn't stop the weight of the cattle as they plowed into it. Wood splintered and suddenly the buffalo were running free.

Mak grinned silently—before realizing that the herd was heading straight for him. He jumped to his feet—startling the buffalo directly in front of him. They veered to the side to avoid the unexpected obstacles and several of them careered into the shack with such force they tore through the flimsy wall.

The animals wheeled away from the collapsing cabin as the kerosene lanterns inside dropped and shattered—immediately igniting the building.

Now highlighted by the burning cabin, Mak was visible. Sunil pointed a finger at him and shouted aggressively. Then the man raised his rifle and fired. It clicked on an empty barrel—his last shot having been a hasty one into the trees.

As the Indian rapidly reloaded, Mak raced away from the burning shack—just as the ammunition in the weapons supply detonated with a colossal *bang*. The chest itself rushed skyward like a flaming rocket before landing in the cabin where the furs were drying. More flames immediately took hold.

The explosion hurled Mak to the ground, and he lay sprawled face-first in the dirt. The noise frightened the buffalo running toward the cabin. As one, the fleeing creatures wheeled around and by the time Sunil had finished reloading and looked up, they were bearing down on him.

Mak could hear only the scream as the man was crushed beneath the hoofs, and when the buffalo finally disappeared into the darkness, there was no sign of Sunil or Gideon.

Mak slowly stood up as the remaining two cabins caught fire. Flames licked high into the air, sending up streams of embers. He looked forlornly at the cabin containing the radio. His only opportunity to call for help was burning merrily in the flames.

He was so lost in thought, that he didn't hear the footsteps until it was too late. Gideon limped from the darkness, dragging his broken leg behind him and using his rifle as a crutch. One side of his body and face was covered in dirt, and he was bleeding from where the stampede had trampled him.

"You little muckraker!" he snarled. "Look what you've done!"

Mak scowled at the man. He had no sympathy for Gideon's injuries and was in no mood to be treated like some naughty schoolkid. Mak was mad with rage.

"You got what you deserved," said Mak through gritted teeth.

"Oh yeah?" Gideon dropped to his knees, grimacing in pain as he did so. "Now you're going to get it too!"

In one deft motion he raised his gun and started to squeeze the trigger.

Mak hadn't been looking at Gideon. At the very last second a blur of movement to the side caught his attention. It was the panther.

The sleek killer was racing toward them at full sprint. The flames, the stampede, and gunshots had meant the creature had been hidden from sight—until now. Only now did it choose to spring into attack mode.

It leaped from the ground, jaws wide and razor-sharp talons extended. The light of the fires seemed to make its beautiful coat shimmer, revealing the fresh scar across its neck, sustained by Gideon's poaching snare.

The panther struck Gideon at full speed a fraction before he pulled the trigger. At almost forty miles per hour, the impact of a sixty-pound cat was enough to break almost every bone in Gideon's body. They tumbled away into the darkness with a roar from the panther and a futile scream from the man, who quickly fell silent as tooth and claw did their work.

CHAPTER FIFTY-SIX

MAK WAS STILL STANDING, shaking, as the panther emerged from the darkness and padded toward him, licking its lips. The noble creature stopped just an arm's length away.

Mak felt a sense of awe at its power and grace. He could see its nose twitching as it took in his scent.

Then, to Mak's astonishment, the cat sat down with its head laid on its front paws as it had done on the log all that time ago. It began to purr, a bass-heavy rumbling noise that reminded Mak of a pneumatic drill. Its big eyes looked imploringly at him, then it purposefully rubbed its neck, scraping the radio collar on the ground.

Mak knew what was expected of him. "I hear you. Just like last time, right?"

Taking one long breath, Mak gently reached for the radio collar, just as he had done with the snare. He made no sudden moves, frightened that the slightest jolt could be misinterpreted as an attack.

The collar was firmly attached and no amount of pulling seemed to dislodge it, and Mak dared not try harder. The cat murmured impatiently.

"I'm trying . . . Stay with me."

His fingers ran along the box that contained the GPS tracker itself. This meant edging closer to the cat, and Mak was all too aware that his tender throat was so close to the panther's mouth that he could feel its every breath.

He experimentally squeezed the tracker and felt something move. Further experimentation found there was a pair of clips on opposite sides of the tracker that when he pressed together and clicked, made the collar slip off.

Even before the collar hit the ground the panther was on its feet, startling Mak so much he fell unceremoniously backward. The animal bounded across the clearing and away into the darkness. Mak fancied he saw a pair of eyes reflected briefly in the flames, lazily blinking in thanks before they too vanished.

Mak felt numb. He had saved the magnificent animal, but without the radio that had been burned, he had no means of calling for help. He was certain that the poachers would never have contacted the outside world.

Then he picked up the GPS collar and examined it. He had hoped it contained a transmitter, something he could push and call for help, but of course it did not. Why would anybody build such a function into something designed solely for tracking movement?

It was useless for Mak's purposes.

He had no options left. Gideon had been evasive when Mak had asked in which direction the nearest town was. He watched the fires send up plumes of black smoke and shook his head; even such obvious smoke signals were useless without anybody in range to see them.

Smoke signals.

Mak looked at the tracker in his hand. This was a digital smoke signal of sorts, *if only somebody was looking.* He craned his head to the clear sky—nothing but stars, the moon, and the lone cloud that had almost disappeared.

Of course! Stars. And satellites.

Mak dashed over to the pen and twisted a piece of the broken gate off its smashed frame. Then he drew a message in the dirt using the largest letters he had the space to create.

Then, holding the tracker aloft, Mak ran as fast as he could, his feet tracing the letters first one way, then back the other. He ran long into the night, retracing the path over and over again until his legs and arms ached and the blazing cabins had collapsed into nothing but smouldering embers.

Only then did he curl up in the dust and fall fast asleep.

He prayed someone, somewhere, was doing their job and watching the tracker device's movements.

CHAPTER FIFTY-SEVEN

Mak's first thought was that another monsoon was about to strike—or worse, a cyclone. He had jolted awake to the sound of continuous thunder and gale-force winds. Now he shielded his eyes as he looked around in panic . . . then tilted his head upward.

A helicopter was hovering overhead, an enormous red-and-white beast with the word "RESCUE" emblazoned on one side.

The downdraft was kicking up a tornado of dust and debris from the fire, forcing Mak to shield his eyes. He moved to the edge of the clearing, keeping close to the trees.

The aircraft slowly descended and the side door rolled open. A man dressed in a red flight suit and wearing a helmet beckoned Mak to approach. Mak's legs felt like jelly as he did so. No sooner did he reach the door than the man's powerful arms scooped him up and hauled him inside.

He heard the man's repeated assurances that he was safe, and that everything would be fine. Mak wasn't really listening. He was staring at his mother and father sitting in the jump-seats opposite, tears streaming down their faces. Even as the helicopter began to rise, they unfastened their harnesses—ignoring the pilot's pleas to stay seated—and rushed to embrace Mak.

With the roar of the engines, Mak couldn't hear what they were saying, but he didn't need to. He was crying; everybody was crying.

It was all that they could do.

MAK STOOD ON THE JETTY of Anil's village, watching as a boat arrived with its precious cargo: a barrel of aviation fuel. It turned out that Mak had been lost so deep in the jungle that the rescue chopper was flying on fumes when they had found him. They had been forced to land at Kangri, even though a special clearing needed to be created just for the purpose, and they had had to wait for it to be refueled.

For Mak, Kangri was a welcome break before the big step back to the city. Anil, Diya, and the villagers had watched in astonishment as Mak had disembarked the aircraft with his parents.

His father had squeezed him until they had both almost passed out, assuring him that he would never doubt his son ever again. That they loved him more than words could ever say.

After a two-hour bath—in which the water turned black and was refreshed four times—and a change of clothes, Mak finally heard the story of how his parents and Anil had survived the tidal bore and managed to upright the boat once they had found it wedged in a snarl of roots.

The poor captain hadn't been so lucky, and they feared Mak had met the same fate.

Search parties had combed the area for two solid weeks, but the wave had been the biggest ever recorded. Despite the ever-increasing size of the search grid, they had seen or found no sign of a survivor.

For two more weeks his parents hadn't given up hope, and his father had used every single GeoTek resource to search for him, but eventually they'd had to stop.

Neither of them had given up hope, but it *had* been almost two months since he disappeared.

It had been a complete shock to Anil to see one signal moving so erratically while he was studying the GPS tracking data on his laptop. When he'd zoomed in on the map, he'd had to call Diya over to confirm he wasn't going crazy.

The tracker was moving rapidly, repeatedly spelling out the message SOS.

It could only mean one thing: someone was communicating with them, and that person was in need of help . . .

CHAPTER FIFTY-EIGHT

ANIL HADN'T WASTED ANY TIME contacting the authorities, leading to Mak's eventual rescue.

Safely back in the village, Mak watched the team unload the fuel barrel onto a cart and roll it toward the parked helicopter. Diya joined him, and tried to act casual and not gawp at him in awe, as she had done every moment since his return.

"Looks as if you'll be leaving soon," she said, as normally as she could. "I bet you're looking forward to never seeing this place again."

Mak cast his eyes over the river and the trees bristling with life. The thought of returning home to London, to the concrete safety of his home and a regular pattern to his days, filled him with . . . dread.

He knew it was silly to miss the danger, but

between the moments of jeopardy there had been truly magical times with friends he would never meet again.

"I'm really going to miss this place," he replied.

If Diya was surprised, she didn't show it. Instead she nodded. "The jungle does that to you, doesn't it?"

Mak smiled at her. "It does."

He noticed the village elder was shambling over. Mak still didn't know how old the man was, but he walked with purpose on his matchstick-thin legs. When he reached Mak he took the boy's hands in his own and spoke, pausing to allow Diya to translate.

"He says the spirit of the jungle has embraced you as its child. It is a gift bestowed on only a few, to those with the heart to survive, not just the strength."

The old man's bony finger tapped Mak's chest to emphasize the point. "It seldom happens," Diya continued. "And when it does, those anointed by the spirit live on in legend."

Mak smiled. "Like Mowgli?"

The old man chuckled, his face transforming into the jolliest smile Mak could ever remember witnessing. Even Diya was surprised by his reaction.

"Yes, like Mowgli," she translated. "Mowgli was my grandfather."

She stopped and stared at the old man.

"Your grandfather?" she asked him, as if confused.

"Yes, my grandfather."

"So he was real?"

The old man nodded and talked with growing enthusiasm. Diya was spellbound and Mak had to nudge her arm to get her attention.

"What's he saying?"

Diya blinked in surprise, remembering her role. "Sorry. He was saying that of course he was real—and that the trees, the river, the animals themselves combine to form the guardian spirit of Mowgli. Perhaps those very animals you encountered were part of the same spirit that made Mowgli who he was."

Mak didn't know what to say. The thought that he was part of a special legacy made him tingle with quiet pride.

Diya continued. "His grandfather was known as Mowgli—'Little Frog.' He now gives you the name *Lupli*." She giggled when she saw Mak frown inquisitively.

"It means 'Little Wolf.'"

"Lupli." Mak liked the sound of it. He nodded. He tapped his chest and said it louder. "Lupli!"

The old man nodded and gave him a toothy smile. Still chuckling, the elder made his way back to the village, pausing only to stop and shout something back at Mak. Whatever it was sent him into further giggles.

"What did he say?"

Diya leaned on the jetty rail and looked across the river thoughtfully before she answered.

"He said the jungle hasn't finished with you yet."

Mak followed her gaze and smiled. His adventure had taught him always to trust his inner voice and never to give up hope. And if the jungle had said that it wasn't finished with him, well, then Little Wolf wasn't finished with it.

And someday he would return.

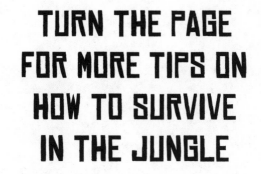

TURN THE PAGE
FOR MORE TIPS ON
HOW TO SURVIVE
IN THE JUNGLE

FINDING WATER

When he is first stranded in the jungle, Mak has to make finding water a priority. He quickly discovers that drinking from a stagnant pool is dangerous and has to search around for other sources of water.

- Collecting rainwater is the quickest and safest way to get hold of drinking water. If you have one, tie a piece of tarpaulin between two trees and wait for the rain to fall. As it collects, you can filter it into a container to use later.

- Large jungle leaves often collect rainwater, which will be fresh to drink. They can also act as funnels to channel water into any containers you're able to find.

- You should always try to purify any water you collect by boiling it over a fire or using purifying tablets if you have them.

FINDING OR BUILDING SHELTER

Shelter is a big priority when you're trying to survive in the jungle. It'll keep you dry, and the best shelters will help to camouflage you from predators.

- Caves are the best kind of natural shelter if you need to get out of the rain quickly, though watch out for bats and other wild animals who may not want to share their home with you!

- Make a simple lean-to by finding a fallen tree with a height of about three feet. Find as many long, straight branches as you can and lay them close together, propped against your tree trunk. Once you have a basic shape, you can cover your tent structure with moss, bark, and branches thick with leaves.

FINDING FOOD

Mak is quickly so desperate for food that he's happy to eat whatever Mother Wolf brings home for her pups. There is plenty of other nutritious food that can be found in the wild, but it's important to be very wary of poisons.

- Bananas, plantains, and coconuts grow abundantly in the jungle and are also a good source of water. Most parts of a palm tree are also edible, but they taste much better cooked.

- Fishing is a great way to have a fresh, cooked meal when outdoors, but fish can be very hard to catch. Making a spear using a long pole with a pointed end is one way to try to catch them, often best done at night.

- Termites are full of protein and taste a bit like nutmeg. If you find a termite mound, get chewing, as a few dozen of these will help keep your energy levels up!

BUILDING A FIRE

Mak finds it very difficult to light a fire in the jungle, but he knows it's essential for survival—for providing warmth, cooking food, boiling water, and even sending up smoke signals.

1. Choose a spot in a clear, sheltered space, a long way from any hanging branches, and dig a shallow hole in the ground.

2. You will need kindling—small, dry twigs—and some leaves as tinder to get you started. Build a pyramid of twigs over your dry leaves, making sure to leave some space for air to circulate.

3. Light your fire—this is the difficult part. If your matches have been washed away in a rainstorm, you can hold a piece of glass with a convex surface (like the bottom of a bottle) up to the light. The heat of the sun's rays will be concentrated through the glass and should provide enough energy to get very fine, dry tinder going.

4. As the smaller twigs burn, gradually add thicker pieces of wood, being careful to make sure it doesn't burn too quickly.

MAKING A RAFT

Mak's journey along the Wainganga River is treacherous but ultimately saves his life, as it leads him back to civilization. The raft he makes is a crucial part of his journey.

The jungle is full of materials you might need to make your raft. The easiest raft to make is a log raft:

1. Find two very sturdy branches, as straight and thick as possible.

2. Tie the logs together with long lengths of vine, leaving about two feet of vine between them. Your logs will now stay tied together, but there will be a space for you to sit in—a makeshift armchair!

3. Use a long, straight branch as an oar to paddle yourself downstream.

Thank you for reading this Feiwel and Friends book.

The Friends who made

SPIRIT OF THE JUNGLE

possible are:

JEAN FEIWEL, Publisher

LIZ SZABLA, Associate Publisher

RICH DEAS, Senior Creative Director

HOLLY WEST, Editor

ALEXEI ESIKOFF, Senior Managing Editor

KIM WAYMER, Senior Production Manager

ANNA ROBERTO, Editor

CHRISTINE BARCELLONA, Associate Editor

KAT BRZOZOWSKI, Editor

ANNA POON, Assistant Editor

EMILY SETTLE, Administrative Assistant

PATRICK COLLINS, Creative Director

ILANA WORRELL, Production Editor

Follow us on Facebook or visit us online at mackids.com.

OUR BOOKS ARE FRIENDS FOR LIFE.